Praise for *Becoming Jane Eyre*

"Sensitive, intelligent and engaging . . . Kohler offers an imaginative recreation of the woman who created this once-scandalous, now beloved classic." —*Kirkus Reviews* (starred review)

"Passionate . . . a novel that refuses to be distracted from the simple but sophisticated act of literary creation." —*The Boston Globe*

"Sheila Kohler moves with assured ease between fiction and biography, between the inner life of Charlotte Brontë as she composes *Jane Eyre* and the comedy of professional rivalry among the three Brontë sisters."

—J. M. Coetzee, author of *Disgrace* and *Summertime*

"Sheila Kohler's imagination—deep and playful, always original—instinctively completes that of her elusive subject, Charlotte Brontë, with such intelligence and perception that we give ourselves over without hesitation." —Susanna Moore, author of *In the Cut*

"An unforgettable journey enriched by a sympathetic understanding of the three Brontë sisters as well as their writing."

—Frances Kiernan, author of *The Last Mrs. Astor*

"Sh
cu

"B
the

"E
ter
lot
rer
an

LOVE CHILD

SHEILA KOHLER

PENGUIN BOOKS

PENGUIN BOOKS
Published by the Penguin Group
Penguin Group (USA) Inc.,
375 Hudson Street, New York, New York 10014, U.S.A. · Penguin Group (Canada),
90 Eglinton Avenue East, Suite 700, Toronto, Ontario, Canada M4P 2Y3 (a division of
Pearson Penguin Canada Inc.) · Penguin Books Ltd, 80 Strand, London WC2R 0RL,
England · Penguin Ireland, 25 St Stephen's Green, Dublin 2, Ireland (a division of
Penguin Books Ltd) · Penguin Group (Australia), 250 Camberwell Road, Camberwell,
Victoria 3124, Australia (a division of Pearson Australia Group Pty Ltd) · Penguin
Books India Pvt Ltd, 11 Community Centre, Panchsheel Park, New Delhi – 110 017,
India · Penguin Group (NZ), 67 Apollo Drive, Rosedale, Auckland 0632, New
Zealand (a division of Pearson New Zealand Ltd) · Penguin Books (South Africa)
(Pty) Ltd, 24 Sturdee Avenue, Rosebank, Johannesburg 2196, South Africa

Penguin Books Ltd, Registered Offices:
80 Strand, London WC2R 0RL, England

First published in Penguin Books 2011

1 3 5 7 9 10 8 6 4 2

PUBLISHER'S NOTE
This is a work of fiction. Names, characters, places, and incidents either are the product
of the author's imagination or are used fictitiously, and any resemblance to actual per-
sons, living or dead, business establishments, events, or locales is entirely coincidental.

LIBRARY OF CONGRESS CATALOGING-IN-PUBLICATION DATA
Kohler, Sheila.
Love child / Sheila Kohler.
p.   cm.
ISBN 978-0-14-311919-7
1. Young women—South Africa—Fiction.   2. Illegitimate children—Fiction.
3. Triangles (Interpersonal relations)—Fiction.   4. South Africa—
History—1909-1961—Fiction.   I. Title.
PR9369.3.K64L68 2011
823'.914—dc22   2011011990

Printed in the United States of America
Set in Bembo • Designed by Elke Sigal

❊

To my mother, Sheila May Bodley Kohler
1908–1984

LOVE CHILD

PART ONE

※

CHAPTER ONE

1956

SOMEONE RINGS HER DOORBELL IN THE HEAT OF THE DECEMBER day. She is lying on her big bed in her silk dressing gown. Who would trouble her on a Sunday at the rest hour?

Her cream curtains are closed on the glare of southern light, the dry, barren veld of the Transvaal. It has been an unusually early and dry summer, and everything is coated with red dust; the smell lingers in the air.

She turns over, ignoring the bell, but her servant, Gladys, has apparently heard it, too. Through her door, open onto the landing at the top of the stairs, she hears Gladys's footsteps, the creak of the front door, and low voices in the hall. Gladys, who comes from the Cape, lives in a small back bedroom, and was undoubtedly resting, too. Despite her advanced age, she has answered the bell with surprising alacrity, almost as if she were waiting for it, and is now padding up the stairs to announce the arrival. Bill—her brother and sisters have always called her that, as she was a tomboy as a child—turns onto her back and half opens her eyes. Gladys leans against the jamb, her hands to her heart, catching her breath.

"Who is it? Tell them to go away," Bill says with a groan.

"Better see him, Madam," Gladys says and shakes her turbaned head disapprovingly. She stands neat and erect in her gray uniform and clean white apron. Bill is not sure of Gladys's age, which she keeps, like most things about her life, to herself. A woman of mixed blood, she has always been closed and silent, keeping her own counsel, and only offering information or advice when asked for it, and even then, sparingly. Like Bill's aunts, whom she worked for with such diligence over so many years, Gladys has never married and never had any children of her own. She has lived her entire life vicariously through these white people.

"It is Mr. Parks," she says, pronouncing the name like porks, Afrikaans being her first language, though she speaks English fluently, as well as a smattering of native languages. She says she will bring coffee and her best shortbread biscuits. "He's waiting in the lounge," she adds, leaving Bill little choice but to rise from her bed.

BY THE TIME BILL ENTERS, the accountant is slumped in the pink armchair in the shadows of her sitting room, nodding a little with post-prandial somnolence, his bald pate shining, and his thick pink lips peeping out rather obscenely from a trim, prim mustache. She remembers, as she sees him rise to greet her, that he had indeed telephoned earlier that week and suggested this visit. She apologizes for the wait.

He murmurs that he hopes he has not disturbed her, looking at her askance. "The matter appears of some urgency," he says, vaguely and pompously.

She supposes he considers her indolent and probably thinks she lives above what he would not hesitate to call, even in 1956, "her station." Perhaps she should have dressed for him. She has brushed her hair and put on lipstick, after all, but remained in her dressing gown, albeit an extravagantly embroidered one of elaborate silk, a bright red kimono, which she bought on a trip to Japan, and her high-heeled slippers, which slap against her heels as she walks over to him. The loose sleeve falls away and shows off her smooth arm as she shakes his dry, plump hand.

For her part she does not like his gray South-African-style baggy trousers and the too-wide jacket, with its padded shoulders, or the way the man is speaking to her in clichés. Of course he has disturbed her, she wants to reply. Why had she agreed to a meeting on a Sunday afternoon? He has always seemed phony and stiff to her, though she knows her husband trusted him and indeed had appointed him the executor of his estate.

"A man of middling intelligence but diligent and, above all, honest," her husband had said. He always said he preferred to hire B students, because they often made good workers, didn't ask too many questions, and caused less trouble than the brainy ones.

When they are seated opposite one another, Mr. Parks tells her without much preamble that he has come to discuss her will. "It is high time you made one," he says firmly.

"Surely there is no rush," she says, surprised, looking into his pale blue eyes.

"I know it's an unpleasant business, but I feel duty bound to see it is done as soon as possible. It's important for you to have a will, now that the estate is settled," he says annoyingly, stirring the cup of coffee with milk that Gladys has apparently felt obliged to offer him.

The amount of the fortune her husband has left her, Mr. Parks reminds her—as if it were necessary—is considerable. She is fortunate. Thanks to her husband's good mind and hard work, she has been left a very wealthy woman.

She does not particularly like to be reminded that her money has come to her through her husband's hard work or that of Mr. Parks, for that matter, who had worked diligently with her husband for so many years and who she understands is not so subtly and rather smugly complimenting himself. It makes her feel uneasy and not a little ashamed to be reminded how rich she has become at her husband's death, propped up by plump cushions, on this smooth love seat she has had covered in pink silk in the lounge of the garden flat with its view of the blue hills which she has rented with the money her husband left her.

She also resents having her household woken up in order to remind her of the inevitability of her own death. Why should she have to contemplate it, at this point in her life, as she listens to her accountant clearing his throat, waiting for her response.

"I assure you I'm in perfectly good health," she says, drawing herself up and sucking in her stomach. Perhaps she should have dressed, after all. She has always prided herself on her good health and is, after all, only forty-eight, her birthday still months away in May.

"I certainly hope so," he says, looking at her rather dubiously. He goes on, "I certainly hope that you are taking good care of yourself and that you will remain in good health for a very long time. You are, some might even say, in the prime of your life." He smiles his little prim smile that somehow seems suggestive to her. He adds, finishing off his coffee and looking down at his empty cup, "However, one can never be absolutely sure, at any age, of what is up ahead, and a will would avoid all sorts of delays and confusion for your heirs."

She watches him stroke his mustache, as though surveying with some satisfaction the trouble that might lie up ahead for her and her heirs. What woman of her age contemplates the writing of a will on a summer afternoon, after eating a large luncheon (several lamb chops, rice, spinach, fruit salad, and ice cream) and drinking several glasses of beer? How can she make up her mind who should inherit what?

Besides, she has never felt at ease with Mr. Parks. He reminds her of a character out of Dickens, though she's not sure which one as it has been a long time since she read the novels. She considers Mr. Parks old-fashioned, pompous, long-winded, and prudish. She doesn't know what he knows about her past. She suspects he has never approved of her entirely, though he has always been excessively polite.

He puts the remains of Gladys's shortbread biscuit down on the plate beside him. With his starched linen napkin, he carefully brushes the crumbs from his mustache and asks her to give it all some serious thought. "Perhaps jot down a list of names and a few sums. I'd be happy to stop by the flat one day next week with the lawyer and draw it up. I don't think you want to delay much longer," he says. "There are the jewels alone to think about, particularly now that your boys are almost grown. Some of the diamonds must be very valuable. Why, the yellow diamond alone is worth a small fortune."

Why is he talking about her jewels and her heirs as though they were legion? She is suddenly suspicious. "I don't think my boys would fight over my jewels," she says haughtily, tossing her head. She cannot imagine such a thing.

"I'm afraid, in my experience, even the best of people are apt to act unpredictably when there's an inheritance," Mr. Parks says.

Once again, there is a long silence after this platitude, while Bill fusses with the cups on the silver tray next to her, trying to look calm, pouring herself and him another cup, holding the ebony handles of the coffee and milk pots at the same time. As he rises to take his cup from her, Mr. Parks looks her in the eye, clears his throat again, and says the matter should be taken care of as soon as possible. It is a simple matter, after all, as he presumes she will surely want to leave most of her money to her two boys. He realizes that this is difficult for her, but it is, after all, now six months since her husband's death.

There is a long pause while she looks back at him, the demitasse with its gilt rim, the tiny silver spoon in his pink palm. Does he, she suddenly wonders, appalled at the thought, expect her to leave something to him? Surely, he wouldn't dare suggest it? It is true he has done well for her husband and has been helpful and obliging to her. Is that why he's being so insistent? She has never been good with figures, which roll away in her mind like the shiny marbles she played with as a child in the dirt with her mother's servant's little boy.

She watches him sit stiffly back down and adjust the pleats of his pants. She says, "I don't know that my boys will need any more money. Their father, after all, left them a good deal already."

"A small portion of a large fortune. I imagine he thought you would leave them the rest at your death," he says.

"I will have to take care of my own family," she says without looking at him. Since her boys have gone away to boarding school, she has relied increasingly on her relatives for company. Despite her wealth and her husband's position, Johannesburg society has snubbed her. She has seen no one except her family, whom she has confided in from an early age. They are the only ones who know her whole story, the guardians of her many secrets.

"Your own family?" he asks, looking bemused.

She remembers now, as she sips from her cup, that she has invited her sisters and brother to lunch the next day.

He brings her back into the moment, leaning toward her slightly in his armchair, plucking at his trouser legs as he says, "Surely your husband would have wanted his money to go to his *own* children." He blinks his white eyelashes over his pale blue, protuberant eyes, pulling down his long upper lip with finger and thumb, stroking his mustache.

She is unable to respond, and her cup shakes in her hands. The curtains, the flowered mauve carpet, the silver tray with its ebony-handled pots, even the Pierneef paintings on the walls, spin around her. For a moment she is afraid she'll fall to the floor.

She wonders what he knows about her. She pulls herself up on her plump pink pillows and takes a gulp from the demitasse, the milky coffee trickling down her chin into the décolleté of her red gown. She wipes it away angrily, then stands up, determined not to let him bully her into any sort of confession. She shall not let him, or anyone else, force her into doing something she doesn't want to do. Great unhappiness comes from letting others interfere.

He looks at the carpet and says, "I would simply suggest that you give all of this careful consideration."

In a haughty tone she says she must really rest as she does at this hour every afternoon, and it is Sunday after all. She thanks him for his advice.

"Advice, as always, given in your best interest," he says in an injured tone as he rises to leave her. She abandons him in the hall, as he takes up his gray hat with the ribbon around the brim, which Gladys brushes off for him carefully.

As Bill goes back up the curving staircase, one hand on the white banister, entering her large bedroom, she hears them conferring in low voices in the hall. She wonders what they might be saying. She hears Mr. Parks murmuring something about Gladys's biscuits and something else she doesn't catch. She enters her bedroom, walks quickly across the soft cream carpet, dark curls in her eyes. She pulls out the center drawer in her dressing table and feels at the back for the secret spring. She pulls out the Craven "A" tin in which she keeps some of her jewels. She feels its weight and heft, and hears the reassuring rattle. She adjusts the lined curtains to shut out the light and lies down on her wide bed, throwing an arm across her face. But she cannot rest. Grief grips her around the neck like a thief.

She thinks of the women in her life: her mother, her three

maiden aunts, Gladys, her sisters, Helen. She has always been surrounded by women who kept secrets in shaded, silent places, but the secrets did not keep them. They wore away at them, worried them from the inside out, and destroyed them, slowly.

Now, one image springs at her after another, coming at her from all directions like wild animals flushed from cover. She remembers so clearly what happened the afternoon her mother told her to fetch her father from his work. She sees them all at that moment in the house on R Street. Though she left it many years ago, she can still see the rooms distinctly: even the dark corridor leading into the kitchen and the back courtyard with the servant's coal fire.

CHAPTER TWO

1925

OFTEN, THEIR MOTHER WOULD SEND ONE OF HER THREE daughters—Pie, Bill, or Haze—to fetch her husband home. She was afraid of large spaces and rarely left the narrow house on R Street, where they all grew up. She spent much of her time in her bedroom on the ground floor, where she lay on her bed with the shutters closed, Haze's big marmalade cat beside her, the door open. She would call out querulously to her children to comfort her. She was afraid of going to town even flanked by her precious girls.

She was the sort of woman who experienced many domestic crises, or what she considered such, and called out for her husband, "Robert! Robert! Where, oh, where is my Rob?" pressing her hands together. If a pipe burst or a servant came in with a bleeding head, or little Charles, her only boy, whom she called Chuckie, said he had a stomachache, one of her girls would he dispatched in haste to take the tram into town to bring her Rob back to her. In those early days there was no telephone.

The small, untidy house was crowded with people. Bill remembers the smell of sweat, Dettol, Jeyes Fluid, and red floor polish, rubbed on by hand. For years the three girls slept in the same hot bedroom under the eaves. She was in the middle bed, the best one, under the window and the fan, the one farthest from the sloping ceiling. Her sisters were slipped under the eaves, like afterthoughts, on either side of her. Their bedroom looked over the small back garden, with wisteria growing up the wall, the dark mulberry tree, her father's rose beds, the servant's room, the coal fire where the servant cooked her mealie meal, and the privy.

Young Charles was in a closet-sized room adjacent to their own, but spent most of his time in theirs, sometimes even sleeping in one of their beds. A small, delicate child, he was often ill, and from the start his older sisters had spoiled him. He was always coming into their room for something he couldn't find: scissors, slippers, even a shirt. He liked to dress up in their clothes or to ask for their help or just to sprawl on their beds and listen to their constant gossip. All three girls loved to talk.

Bill's parents slept in the narrow double bed on the ground floor, or, more often, their father slept on a leather sofa next door in the lounge, which doubled as a dining room if there was company. Mostly, the family was crammed noisily and uneasily into the kitchen, which had been added on at the back of the house, where the table had its soiled checked tablecloth and the bowl of overripe fruit with the fruit flies hovering, the windows dirty, and the linoleum scuffed. The three girls bathed altogether at length in the one big bath, talking away in the only bathroom.

Their mother kept one slovenly drudge of a servant who was both untrained and overworked. She polished the red tiled floors on the front verandah and then did the whole family's laundry by hand, starting at the break of day. Their mother told the story of advising the servant to wash her hands after using the privy. She protested, "But I never touched nothing, Madam!"

The small servant's room was adjacent to the privy, with its double seat, where the girls could sit together and chat as they strained over their stools. There was no privacy. Bill remembers pretending to be a witch, making scary noises to frighten Haze, the youngest girl, threatening to come up from the hole below and steal her private parts. "I'm coming to take your winky away," she would say in a high falsetto voice.

From morning to night, the doors would swing open from one room to the next, and the walls were thin. The children could hear their mother weeping at night.

Their mother had been a spoiled, dreamy, pretty girl in her youth, with thick hair and small hands and feet she was proud of, who had never been taught to cook or clean or fend for herself, she told them. She was incapable of saving money, keeping her accounts in order, or making sure she wasn't cheated in the shops. She lacked organizational skills and had difficulty getting out of bed in the morning, so she relied on her daughters to fulfill her role. She could not be left alone for long.

Bill's father told her in confidence one day, when she was hardly ten years old: "You must help your mother, she has never really learned to cope with a household of children."

Their father had definite ideas on many subjects and could be extremely stubborn when aroused, particularly in the case of his favorite daughter, Bill. A meek, unambitious, and reasonable man, a good father and devoted, faithful husband, who worked hard in the diamond business to support his large family, he never drank more than one glass of beer with dinner and loved his roses, which he tended and watered diligently, always muttering that no one should grow them in Africa, it was too difficult. Yet he had known how to get Bill to do what he wished.

She doesn't remember what the emergency was that time, just her mother calling her forth as she lay on her bed in her gown, eating sweets and chatting with Pie after lunch. She remembers groaning with annoyance, telling Pie to go instead. But it was Bill her mother wanted. "Bill, come and brush my hair," she would say, or "Rub my back, won't you, darling heart?" which she maintained Bill could do more soothingly than the others.

Bill stood in the doorway of her mother's room and asked what she wanted now. Her mother told her to put on her coat and hat and go and get Papa. "Hurry! Hurry, pet!" she urged.

"Hold your horses," Bill replied.

It was a chilly day in August, not long after the Prince of Wales had come out to South Africa and caused such a stir in her household, where English royalty was held in high esteem, their smallest actions followed with great interest. Bill had seen a newsreel of the handsome young prince, riding in his car and watching a native dance.

Bill's father spoke of England as home, though he had

never been there. It was his grandmother, Miss Pritchard, who had come out to South Africa with the 1820 settlers, as a governess. Bill had seen a photo of the woman on her father's dresser, looking grim in a bonnet. She came from Cornwall in the southwest of England.

Bill's father looked down on the Afrikaners, whom he considered peasants of low extraction and little breeding, and who spoke a language without formal grammar, a sort of bastardized Dutch. He believed they lived in houses with mud floors, committed incest on their isolated farms, and beat the natives with *shambocks*. He was appalled when Hertzog's Nationalists won the elections in 1924, beating Smuts, who had supported the English-speaking mine-owners and whom he admired despite his Boer background.

But Bill, at seventeen, was not particularly interested in her origins, her father's past, his grandmother, or even her own. She was interested in the present or the future, one of her own making which would be quite different. She dreamed of something new and strange entering her hum-drum, sheltered existence. She wanted excitement, even danger. She was restless and reckless. She wanted to fall in love.

Reluctantly she ran to catch the tram to go into town, as she had done so many times before. She knew her father would be reluctant to come home. She ran along Main Street, through the front door of his office building, and up the stairs. The guard smiled when she said she had come to get her father. "Again," he said and opened the door for her to the big room where her father toiled with the other dia-mond evaluators, all of them doing painstaking, meticulous work day after day. Using loupes, they peered down at large piles of stones, sorting them fast. Her father had told her many stories about famous diamonds found in the Premier Mine in Johannesburg, about how they had once thrown the huge uncut Cullinan around the room like a tennis ball.

He said it was work where you had to be constantly vigilant, must never make a mistake, and might experience the thrill of finding something extraordinary. She imagined he was good at his work, a careful, scrupulously honest, hardworking man with an eye for gemstones.

He was not the only one who looked up from his diamond as she came into the room and stood against the door, surveying this crowd of working men. She knew she was the prettiest of her father's three girls, with her large, luminous eyes; dark, soft curls; and slender ankles and tiny feet and hands. She felt particularly pretty, in her pink cloche hat, pulled down slightly to one side, and sling-back shoes. Her narrow brown coat showed off the slim figure she had acquired by starving herself for several months.

A winter's day in the *highveld*, the light gold. She stood at the entrance to the large room with its smell of dust and sunlight, and the low hum of masculine voices, looking from one man to the next. She smiled at her father, who smiled back but did not get up. No doubt he was in no hurry to go home and face whatever calamity awaited him there. Nor was she.

She was aware of the bright sunlight, of Isaac, sitting among the others, along the wall by the window. His red head and beard caught in a beam of light, he was staring down intently at the pile of diamonds before him. But what she noticed most was the way he was moving his hands so fast and continuously, and especially his long adroit fingers.

Pie had already told her in a whisper that she had overheard him talking to their father when she had gone to the office to fetch him. "He has the sweetest voice," she had reported. "I could fancy him, but he may be Jewish, and in that case, Papa would never approve."

Bill had heard her father say contradictory things about Jews. Sometimes, he spoke of them with a certain grudging admiration. "He was one of the Chosen People," he would say ironically of some businessman like Barny Barnato, who had been a partner with Cecil Rhodes and made so much money. He laughed about "Hoggenheimer," the caricature of the rich randlord, who was known to hoard his money. He called the act of successful bargaining "Jewing someone down," and seemed somewhat afraid of their influence. He talked of Johannesburg as becoming Jewburg, inundated with Jewish immigrants who could never be assimilated, spoke a different language, and often kept to themselves, walking around with long beards and little black hats on their heads. At the same time, he acknowledged that they were the ones who maintained the cultural life of the city, the music and paintings and theater—the little there was then.

To her they seemed exotic and a little dangerous—forbidden, and therefore enticing. She walked over to Isaac's desk and perched recklessly on the edge of it, dangling her legs. He looked up and smiled at her. She removed one of her shoes, showing off her small, slender ankle and foot, the nails painted a bright orange.

She said, "Sorry," and pretended to remove something from her shoe. Then she stood up and adjusted the angle of her hat. He went on staring at her, and boldly she stared back at his thick red hair, worn rather long and curling around his narrow face. She liked the mysterious, hooded dark green eyes, the fine arch of the nose, his freckled, creamy skin, and sensuous mouth.

He must have known whose daughter she was, though to look at her—small, curly-headed, and shapely—she could have been one of his sisters. He must have known she would not have been welcome in his home nor would he, despite his athletic build, his red gold locks, his musical voice, and the poetry he knew by heart, be welcomed in hers.

The light behind him caught the red in his thick hair and beard and the soft, shiny material of his gray waistcoat, clinging to his broad chest. She kept staring into his eyes a moment longer, before saying, casually, as though they had been introduced, "So long." As she walked toward her father, in a neat straight line, swinging her hips a little, crossing the dusty room filled with men stooped over their dull tasks, the room seemed transformed into a bright and busy place, an Oriental bazaar, ablaze with light and life.

Her father looked up and said, "Why, if it isn't my kitten, come to fetch me. Some trouble at home?" He spoiled her, often bringing her little treats he knew she loved: a box of her favorite chocolates, a full-blown rose from his garden, a gay ribbon for her glossy hair. It was the last time they walked out of the office together, arm in arm.

CHAPTER THREE

🎇

1956

SHE WONDERS NOW WHAT SHE SHOULD TELL HER FAMILY. PER-
haps she should not mention the will. Perhaps Mr. Parks is
right, and she should leave her fortune to her two boys, now
fifteen and seventeen, though her husband has already left
them a small trust to pay for their education. Still, Mr. Parks
is undoubtedly right: her husband earned that money and
would have expected her to leave it to them.

She misses both her boys terribly. At an early age they
had asked to be sent to an expensive boarding school, and
her husband had thought it a wise choice. But she remembers them as little things, escaping their nanny and padding
into her big bedroom in their white pajamas, their feet bare,
their white blond hair tousled, their skin warm and perfumed, still half asleep, when her husband had left the house
in the early mornings and she was having her breakfast in
bed. She would let them take her jewels from their secret
drawer and climb up on her bed and spill them into her
rumpled sheets with the bread crumbs. She would put the

jewels on their little fingers and toes and intertwine them in their hair. She would gather them up onto her lap and sing to them: "Rings on their fingers and bells on their toes, they shall have music wherever they go." They looked very lovely to her as they lay there, laughing, in the sunlight.

Now she looks at the diamond-studded face of her gold watch on the table beside her. If she hurries, she may arrive in time for Sunday evensong at their school, when the parents are allowed to linger for half an hour or so afterward in the garden to chat with their children. Of course, she should be there. Why had she not thought of this before? She will dress and have the chauffeur drive her there immediately. She will take her boys something to eat, as well, though she's not supposed to. The food is terrible at the school, and the growing boys are always hungry.

She puts her head over the white banister at the top of the stairs and calls for Gladys. After a moment she hears her slow steps and panting on the stairs again. She waits for the old woman in her bedroom.

Bill would have sent her off long ago with a pension, but Gladys has refused to leave. Apparently, she prefers to remain in Bill's large, comfortable garden flat, in the safety of her small back bedroom, which she keeps immaculate with starched white doilies on the back and arms of the armchair and on the dresser, and a large black Afrikaans Bible on the table by her narrow bed, and her two canaries, Paul and Gezina, named for Paul Kruger and his second wife, in their white cage. She emerges from her room in the morning if Bill needs help with dressing, and retreats most afternoons to her room with her sewing and a couple of Marie biscuits for her dinner. Bill is always amazed at how little she eats. Occasionally, a tall, plump nephew visits her on a Sunday afternoon and sits, grinning, in the kitchen on a stool, his hat in his hands, speaking to her in Afrikaans. He drinks tea from a tin mug and stuffs himself with Gladys's best short-bread biscuits and then goes off, no doubt with much of her wages.

Bill asks her now to bring her good mauve silk suit, her leghorn hat with the wide brim and the flowers, and her pink kid gloves with the buttons, and to help her dress. She will go to the chapel service at the school, and she must hurry, or she'll be late. Gladys helps her tug and pull up her elastic lace-and-bone corset and then settle it down over her hips, latch her stockings onto her suspenders, slip on her high-heeled shoes, lift the silk suit over her head, hook her pearls at the back of her neck, settle her hat at the appropriate angle on her head, and puff a little powder on her nose. At the last minute, Bill tells her to give her the large yellow diamond earrings in the shape of stars from her secret drawer, because the boys used to say they looked like daisies.

"Very beautiful," Gladys says, perspiring a little and ad-miring her handiwork, looking at Bill with proprietary pride, as though she is personally responsible for her beauty, her elegance, her life altogether; indeed, Bill considers she is responsible for all of that. She thanks her for her help and, on an impulse, despite her large hat, leans forward to give the old servant a kiss on her remarkably smooth cheek.

She leaves Gladys to straighten up her bed and goes downstairs. She enters the large, sunny kitchen to see what the cook might have for her to take to her boys. There is a delicious odor of roasting chickens.

"Are they cooked?" she asks the tall, ancient Zulu, but he does not deign to reply, only muttering something under his breath. Sometimes she feels he's more trouble than he is worth, grumbling and rude to the two servants. He fights particularly with Gladys, who knows all the secrets of her early life.

The cook is sometimes rude even to Bill, though he adores her boys. Half blind, he sometimes puts sugar instead of salt on the roasts. He speaks very little English, though he has been with her for many years. He looks doubtful and cross at the moment, fussing over the stove, moving around the kitchen, swiping with abrupt, blunt gestures at the countertops with a rag, his starched uniform rustling. He has a mind of his own. He is making a point of preparing early for the Monday luncheon, to which she has told him all her family will be coming. He has little patience for her sisters and particularly for her brother, whom she knows he regards as a meddler, a usurper, and a sponger.

He just stares back at Bill, brittle and dignified, stubbornly guarding his oven—his territory, arms crossed. She elbows him aside, opens the oven, and peers in. The chickens look plump, golden brown, and juicy. "They look perfect to me," she says and tells him she wants to take half a chicken to the boys.

At the mention of them, his expression changes. He shakes his head slowly and sorrowfully, as he always does when she speaks of them. He says something that sounds like, "The poor *n'kosasaan*." He has never approved of their being sent away, and he worries that they are not given enough to eat there, and will grow too thin. Indeed, they seem to her to have grown rather skinny, particularly Phillip, the younger one. She can count his ribs when he takes off his shirt.

The cook spears the larger chicken and holds it aloft, letting the fat run off into a pan. She protests, saying there will not be enough to eat tomorrow and that half of the smaller one would be fine, but he shakes his head and wraps it up carefully.

He has walked her boys to the school bus, carrying their satchels like *assegais* on his shoulders, looking out for *skelms*. He has taken them to the bottom of the garden and told them exciting tales about the military might of the Zulu army and its great battles. They know all about Shaka and his half-brother Dingane, about the Weenen massacre.

He says he'll think of something good to serve for luncheon on Monday. Now he insists on wrapping up a few roasted potatoes as well and slips some sweet-cakes into the wicker basket.

As the chauffeur drives her down the road, the car filled with delicious odors, she feels suddenly lighthearted. She will surprise them, and they will be excited to see her. They will eat together at the bottom of the school garden after church. She salivates at the thought of eating in the company of her boys, and perhaps some of the other starving boarders, of sharing her food, spreading good things around her. It has been such ages since she saw them, held them in her arms, and heard them laugh with pleasure. They are all the world to her. She is even a little afraid of them. She fears that, like

Mr. Parks, they may not entirely approve of her. They are only allowed out every two weeks during the term for a brief Sunday at home when the cook will stuff them with food, and she will try to get them to lie out and relax in the sun without their books.

Suddenly, everything seems simple: she will call Mr. Parks's office tomorrow and tell him she will do as he advises. Of course, she will leave her money to her boys. They will divide the jewels and what is left of the furniture in two without anyone's help. She has always told them everything she has in the world is theirs, and that she lives only for them. She does not need to mention her will to her relatives or anyone else. She will continue to keep it a secret from them and she will insist Mr. Parks does so, too, and when she dies—surely she will not die for ages—she will not care what they think. Perhaps she should confide in her boys one day, or at least tell them something about her past life. Perhaps they would understand. They might even find her story romantic if she tells it right and leaves out a thing or two.

She tells the chauffeur to hurry. She does not want to arrive late for evensong. It is almost twilight now. The golden light and a pink cloud of pollution hover over the city. They are caught up in Sunday afternoon traffic. Night falls so fast here, and it is suddenly almost the end of the day, a sad time, not one she likes.

She sees a young black girl standing like an omen in the twilight by the side of the road, her cup raised beseechingly, and she remembers how she once promised Phillip, who has such a tender heart, to give something to every beggar she saw. She has the chauffeur stop and opens her window to hand over a sixpence and a sweet-cake from the basket. She notices the child's cracked, dusty feet, her ragged dress.

Suddenly, as though descended from the darkling sky, there is a flock of small beggars, beating up the dust with bare feet and pressing against the car door, clamoring for coins. She winds up the window fast, and they bang loudly, threateningly on the pane with their sticky little fists. "Step on it," she says and the chauffeur does not need to be told twice. She looks through the back window at the crowd of hungry children standing like small ghosts that disappear in the twilight dust.

CHAPTER FOUR

✢

1925

SHE STILL SEES ISAAC, TALL, SLENDER, STRONG, AND SO YOUNG, not much older than she is at seventeen, standing in the moonlight, looking up at the window, arm raised, about to throw another pebble or perhaps even a clod of earth at the window pane of the back bedroom on R Street. She lifted the window, put her head out, and waved to him.

She had lain awake and dressed under the covers all evening, her small suitcase already packed and hidden in the closet. She waited for Isaac's soft tap on the window, and sprang up immediately, while her sisters slept heavily on either side of her.

She slipped out of the back bedroom window, out into the warm, moonlit October night, her thin dress flapping wildly around her calves, her diaphanous scarf wound around her head, high-heeled shoes and her cardboard suitcase thrown to the ground, shimmying fast down through the wisteria, falling into a bed of her father's roses and the outstretched arms of her waiting lover. She tried not to giggle when his beard scratched her cheek. He kissed her and picked up her case, and she slipped on her shoes, and together they hurried in the dark to the waiting car.

He had persuaded his older cousin first to teach him how to drive and then to lend him his car, a blue, open Chevrolet. The cousin had taken them out in it on weekends, when they had escaped the city with a group of wild young people, all packed in, driving together to the Vaal river to go frolicking, swimming, and picnicking under the weeping willows on the banks of the river.

Now the car bumped along in fits and starts. Though the cousin had tried to teach Isaac how to drive, or so he had told Bill, he seemed to have difficulty, in his excitement, controlling the pedals and the wheel, all the while keeping one arm around her shoulders, holding her close and turning his head to talk to her.

Isaac, she had discovered in their few secret meetings, liked to talk. He had a great faith in words and was much better read than she: he had read the classics. He had impressed her immensely once, swinging his arm over the back of the seat of the car, accidentally poking his elbow in her eye, as he said he preferred Russian literature to French, as though he had read all of both of them. "The Russians," he said in his low sweet voice, "really have a soul." She wept from the blow to her eye and the thought of him reading all those beautiful books. All she had read was nineteenth-century English literature written by women and not very much of that, either.

He was full of ideas and strong opinions on various subjects and loved to hold forth at length on world history—

particularly South African history, comparing the relative merits of Jan Smuts and Hertzog, as though he knew them intimately. He was particularly interested in Rhodes, who had known his father and whom he admired.

Even at this moment, he was talking, telling her about his narrow escape from his house, complaining of his sisters' endless and frivolous conversation and his mother's solicitude at the dinner table, and his cousin's late arrival, which had delayed him. "I thought I would never get away," he said. He was "kvetching" as he put it, and not concentrating on the road.

From time to time she was obliged to grasp the wheel and spin it, to avoid another car or the ditch. With his long gray scarf fluttering wildly around his thin neck, he was driving far too fast and weaving, both of them laughing aloud exultantly in the moonlight. Despite her father's injunctions, her mother's eternal complaints, her sisters' watchfulness, and despite his clinging sisters, his anxious mother, all the absurd prejudice on both sides, they had managed to get away.

He had asked her to marry him the very first time they had been alone. After his first glimpse of her in the office, he had sent a letter to her house, telling her he had to see her again. She was to meet him at the Zoo Lake. She had liked his tone of authority.

She found him waiting there by the water under a birch tree, the bark white against his silhouette. He was standing on one foot, leaning against the slender tree, wearing a dark beret that was too big for him and did not suit him. For a moment she was disappointed in his appearance. But then they walked along the edge of the lake in the shadow and flickering light of the warm spring evening. Soft clouds drifted across the evening sky like pink balloons. There was a band playing and on all sides people were running about, talking, and laughing. Children were eating cotton candy, and there was a smell of burned sugar. A plump little girl ran into her legs and fell to the ground, and she picked her up and brushed her off. All the time, Isaac seemed to be looking at her with joy and tenderness and perhaps a hint of laughter in his eyes which looked almost light green in the twilight. Then he stopped walking, took off his beret, and put his hand to his head, running it through his thick red curls. "I want to marry you," he blurted out.

"How can I possibly marry you? I don't know you at all, and besides Father would never allow it," she said, laughing.

"We will have to elope then," he said, rashly, recklessly, but as though it were the most ordinary and practical thing in the world. It was his aplomb that thrilled her.

"Elope!" she said, so delighted that she had thrown her arms around his neck and kissed him on the lips. But she had not really believed they would be able to carry it out.

They had seen one another only a few more times. The day before he had announced, "Marvin's going to lend us the car for tomorrow night. I'll be there around ten. Will your family be asleep?"

She nodded. "'Early to bed, early to rise, makes a man healthy, wealthy, and wise,' my father says." She laughed.

But it was later than that when he arrived.

Now it was a wonder that some policeman did not stop them for reckless driving before they had hardly begun their voyage. Fortunately, there were few cars on the road that led down from Johannesburg to the northern Cape and even fewer policemen.

She was delighted to be on the road, going somewhere—anywhere—with Isaac, free of the burden of her family: the crowded house on R Street, her sisters' jealousy, her mother's eternal complaints, her father's short, sharp footsteps when he came in the door every evening with his "Where's my favorite girl, my kitten? Where's my kiss?"

Looking up at the vast African sky, she was crazy with exultation. How bright the thick stars were, spread above her: Orion with his jeweled belt so clear, the Big Dipper. Never had a night sky seemed quite that full of flickering mothlike stars. How brightly the moon lit up the veld stretching away forever into the freedom of darkness.

Toward midnight, the car overheated and sputtered to a complete halt on a deserted stretch of dust road.

"We'll have to go and get some water for the engine," Bill said, having heard about these things. Isaac looked around at the endless sea of flat cornfields and said, "Nothing but mealies around here."

She pointed out the flickering lights of a farmhouse in the distance.

"I'll go and ask for help," Isaac said.

She was afraid he would lose himself in the corn, but he told her to stay and guard the precious car, their "Chariot of Fire." He was always quoting inappropriate lines of poetry. "Brightness falls from the air, Queens have died young and fair, dust has closed Helen's eyes, I am sick, I must die," he would recite.

"Besides, in your high-heeled shoes!" he said, now staring at them disapprovingly. "You should have worn *takkies*!" though she saw he was wearing his best shoes.

"How could I elope in *takkies*!" she protested.

By the time he returned, it was late, and they were now tired and hungry. They had been too excited to eat all that day. When they saw hotel lights on the main square in a small *dorp*, he drew over, managed to stop the car near the curb, gathered her up in his arms and bent down and kissed her on the lips.

"Shall we go in?" he asked, and she did not hesitate at all.

CHAPTER FIVE

1925

"I'M NOT SURE THAT I HAVE ANY ROOMS LEFT," THE BALDING man behind the desk said, regarding them through his one good eye.

Isaac said in his sweet voice, "We'll take whatever you've got. We don't need much room, we've just been married," and waved a fine hand, smiled his charming, spoiled-boy smile, showing small almost transparent teeth. The clerk looked at the two of them and then down at the large black book before him. "Congratulations," he said in a funereal voice which made them grin at one another.

"I might have one small one," he said, "but there's no private bath, the toilet is at the end of the hall, and you'll have to pay in advance."

"Of course," Isaac replied grandly, as if it were nothing to him, pulling out his thin wallet and carefully counting out the exact amount, starting with the coins and then the bills. Bill could hardly wait to lie down beside him. She knew that they had both wanted to touch each other's young, slender, smooth bodies freely, ever since they had met three months before. Their meetings had always been brief and furtive. Neither of them had dared to invite the other home.

They boldly signed the register as a married couple, while the clerk stood in the shadows watching them. He unhooked the wooden bulb of the heavy key and held it in his hand, considering, hesitating. "It's at the top of the stairs," he said discouragingly with a vague wave, without offering to carry any luggage or show them the way.

"The key, please," Isaac said firmly, and the man handed it over to them.

Then Isaac, playing the *grand seigneur*, ordered something to be brought up to the room. "We'd like some dinner, too," he said.

"Don't you think it's a bit late—it's after one o'clock," the clerk grumbled, looking at his gold fob watch. "I don't think anything is available at this hour," he said. "You're lucky you still found me awake!"

Isaac, an only boy and the eldest child, with doting, elderly parents and two adoring sisters, was used to getting his way. He looked down at the man and urged, "Surely there must be something in the kitchen even if it's cold. Be a good man and bring us some cold beers, too, will you?"

They groped their way, giggling, to the top of the dark, dusty stairs, and Isaac turned the large key in the lock with some difficulty. He struggled with the low door, thrusting his shoulder hard against it, nearly falling into the room. Obliged to stoop, he turned on the lamp by the bed. They sat side-by-side on the narrow bed pushed up against the wall, the small, high window slanting above them in the sloping ceiling of the tiny attic room. A small table stood by the bed with a lamp and a cruet of water in a blue and white basin.

Bouncing on the bed like children on a trampoline, they giggled at their daring, ridiculous words, the clerk's absurd, surprised expression, the wild adventure, the fun of it all, waiting to see what would happen next, and what would actually appear in the way of food. They turned suddenly grave and dignified, straightening up their rumpled clothes, when they heard a knock on the door. Isaac sprang off the bed on long legs, knocking his head on a beam, and opened the door on the clerk, who staggered in with his laden tray. "I hope this will do," he said sourly, panting.

"It will do very well," Isaac proclaimed, giving him an extravagant tip.

Once the door closed, they dissolved again into giggles and threw themselves on the food, bolted the big, cold sausages, the hard boiled eggs, and thick slices of brown bread and cheese, feeding one another with fingers and guzzling all the beer.

When they had eaten and drunk everything provided, Isaac put the tray on the dusty floor, pushed it under the bed, and lay down by Bill's side. Shyly, hardly daring to look at first, he helped her take off her clothes, starting with the high-heeled, sling-back shoes.

She will always remember his long, slim legs, in his funny red underwear. Despite the warmth of the October night, he was, for some reason, wearing it, making her think of a long-legged devil. He put his hand on her shoulder and then on her breast and said, "Such beautiful breasts," and she looked down and saw they were, indeed, quite beautiful, and she felt then, looking at herself, desire for him. He said, touching first one and then the other, "Now this is my breast and this is mine, too," and he leaned down and took her nipple in his mouth.

They laughingly explored one another's damp, hot bodies, fumbling around inexpertly. Neither of them had done this before. At first, in her fear, she tightened up so much that he was unable to enter her. He lay panting beside her, for a while, as if stunned, at a loss. "I don't seem very good at this," he said, red in the face, undone, she could see even in the faint light of the bedside lamp, which she had insisted they keep lit. Then she felt pity for him and she loved him more in his shame and was moved to help and encourage him onward, to protect him, to restore his faith in himself. Shyly guided by his hand, she consented to touch what she had never touched before. He tried once again, this time with less confidence, slowly and shyly pressing gingerly against her. Now, giggling at his sheepish expression and no longer so afraid, she was taken off guard. This more subtle approach worked, and he was able to slip in surreptitiously where a more direct attack had failed. Somewhat shaky and exhausted, he was not able to take advantage of the opportunity to drive too deeply. Indeed he was obliged to retreat until she grasped him and encouraged him, pulling him closer, pressing with her legs against his firm, childlike buttocks, which moved her to make him her own. He kept looking into her eyes with gratitude and tenderness until she felt with him the glorious surge, as he accomplished what he had set out to. Then she dared to turn on her side and to show him how to caress her from behind and encouraged him to slip what was left of his manhood into her and stroke her softly until she came, too.

CHAPTER SIX

✣

1925

THEY KEPT GOING ALONG THE DREADFUL ROAD WITH ITS POT-holes and ditches all through the next afternoon, raising dust and scaring sheep as they went, and singing raucously to the blanched blue sky above, to the sparse brown scrub, to the tattered camelthorn trees around them.

The sun was low in the sky when he said, "Is that Kimberley there in the kopjes?" indicating a scatter of buildings which seemed thrown down randomly by a mad god on the veld, surrounded by blue gray hills.

"Yes, but those little blue hills are actually mine dumps," she said, recognizing the place where her father and his three sisters were born. She remembered the diamond town from happy holiday visits with her parents as a child, getting on the train at night and sleeping on a top bunk with her teddy bear clutched to her cheek.

As they entered the confusing, meager streets, some with grand names—Milner and Gladstone and Lyndhurst, and others with common ones like Dump, Muck, and Old Mine Street—she became confused, no longer sure she could find her way to her aunts' house. They drove around in circles.

"What a dreary place! So much corrugated iron," he said as they came simply to barbed wire with nothing but the pale veld beyond. What were they doing here, she wondered, in these half-deserted streets, which she had remembered from her childhood as bustling with life and industry. She was hot and thirsty, and her thighs were still sticky. She had not been able to wash properly at the hotel. The sun was in her eyes.

They came to Market Square which all the streets seemed to run into without making right angles. The houses looked useless rising above To Let signs on the almost empty square.

"It all looks so different. Yet my father said this was the first city in Africa to get electric light," Bill said as they went down the silent streets and passed a dismal, sandy park with a wrought iron gate, an empty bandstand, and a stone statue of Queen Victoria. They came to a monument that Bill remembered had been put up by Cecil Rhodes to honor the dead during the siege of the city.

On her aunts' sloping street, finally, Bill looked out for the house, which she remembered as having a small tidy garden where the aunts grew flowers and their own vegetables.

"There it is! Turn there!" she said, spotting the white picket fence, shaded by a fig tree at the end of a dimly lit cul-de-sac. "That's their garden," she said as they drove down the street in the long shadows of twilight, pointing out the front garden with its neat beds of old-fashioned spring flowers: white Shasta daisies, snapdragons, pinks, daffodils, and early sweet-heart roses growing along the fence.

"They live there?" Isaac said, sounding surprised again. Had he expected something larger, more prosperous, she wondered, suddenly seeing the house through a stranger's eyes. Perhaps all her talk of her grandfather and his will had made Isaac expect something grander.

She had told him about her three maiden aunts whom she remembered with much affection. They had always adored their favorite niece, their beloved brother's most beautiful and lively girl. They had spoiled her, loved to brush her thick hair, to make her pretty dresses, to tell her tales about their cloistered lives, their father's fear of fortune hunters, in the diamond town, his harsh will, which had shackled them together, unable to marry without relinquishing their small estate, how they had suffered but had always been determined to stay together to protect one another, to put the three of them above the good of any one of them, spurning the suitors, one after the other, who had flocked to their house, sent by their cousins who hoped to inherit their money and their house.

Indeed, the house looked smaller and darker than she remembered it. With the reality of her aunts' modest dwelling with its white net curtains in the windows and the low painted green corrugated iron roof before her, the "sanitary lane" behind, she wondered again if she had chosen the best place for them to hide. What had driven her to choose this place, this city which had once seemed so special, a place to make fortunes that now seemed half dead to her?

She saw something stir behind the net curtains, a hand lifting a laced edge, and a pale face glimmering at them. What would her aunts say when they saw them? she wondered now, and her knees felt suddenly watery, her hands moist, her mouth dry.

CHAPTER SEVEN

※

1956

As her car approaches the school, Bill stares out the window and sees a group of younger boys out for a walk in their navy school blazers, short gray pants, long socks, and heavy lace-ups, gray caps on the back of their heads, marching, pink-faced and sweating, in double file down the road. Poor things, she thinks, they must be awfully hot and uncomfortable in school uniforms. She is not quite sure why her boys asked her to send them as boarders to this place, where she knows they still cane boys, giving them "six of the best" for what seem to her minor offenses. Not that her good boys have ever needed caning.

Not much of use, it seems to her, is taught here. Latin and Greek are still required for all the boys and much of the literature and history is confined to the nineteenth century. As they drive up the long, oak-shaded driveway toward the bright white wings of the Dutch gabled building glinting in the twilight, she looks at her watch and realizes she will be late for evensong. She remembers how the French master keeps trying to get her to give money to one of his charities which she is quite convinced has nothing to do with charity. Perhaps, after all, as much as she longs to see her boys, she should never have come.

She hurries through the side gate and down the stone steps into the terraced garden and on to the chapel in the back, carrying her heavy basket with its odor of roasted chicken and potatoes, wobbling a little on the stones in her high heels. As she hears the heavy wooden chapel door clang behind her, she feels a terrible weight and fears she might weep.

The service has begun, the first hymn already underway. "Now the day is over / Night is drawing nigh, / Shadows of the evening steal across the sky," the boys sing too slowly and lugubriously, one of them accompanying the singing on the upright piano and making a mistake from time to time.

What is she doing here? Will her boys even want to see her? She is not sure that they approve of her—they judge people by their tastes, telling everyone they will never marry a girl who does not love Mozart, while she herself never listens to classical music.

Pictures of her early life flood her mind again with all the shame, sadness, and confusion of irreparable loss. She is uncertain of what she should do now, trapped in this hot, closed space. She must close the curtain on the past, draw the shutters down, keep her secrets. She must make an effort, at least for her boys. She must be strong for them.

She walks along the center aisle in the crowded, stuffy chapel with its odors of incense and sweat and its blue murals of a boat and fishermen at sea, and the two identical silver bowls of stiff pink carnations—a flower she has never liked—on the altar. She spots a small space by a window and makes her way along the pew. People turn to stare disapprovingly as she wedges herself along the length of the row with her wide-brimmed hat and her basket.

She sits down with a little thud and notices a young man at her side. He wears a hand-knit gray cardigan, a black polo-neck shirt, and gray trousers pleated at the waist. His fair hair is carefully brushed back from a high, white forehead, and his thick tortoiseshell-rimmed glasses glint at her. His thin lips are pale, as are his cheeks. Probably the math teacher, Bill thinks, fresh out from England, whom Phillip admires tremendously for some reason that is not at all apparent to her.

She fumbles to find the page and in her haste drops the heavy hymnbook on the stone floor and then, to make up for her late entrance and all the clatter, stands up with a rustle and opens her mouth wide to sing the verse lustily. "Comfort those who suffer, / Watching late in pain, / Those who plan some evil, from their sin restrain."

The young man beside her glares at her from the corners of his white-lashed eyes with a glint of disapproval as though she might be planning something sinful. Bill can see the man does not approve of her attire or her singing. Perhaps the precious diamond earrings are a bit much for this place.

She ignores him and cranes her neck to find her two boys. The schoolboys are all sitting in pews nearer the altar in their long-sleeved Sunday-white chapel shirts, navy blazers, and striped ties. Some of them are in the choir stalls. She cannot spot her darling boys. For a moment of panic she thinks she cannot recognize them in the crowd. They all look identical:

slim from spending all their afternoons running around the hockey field or playing rugby or swimming up and down the pool, without being given much to eat; sunburned, and mostly blond South African boys with bland, even features. Then she spots one on the other side of the aisle in the choir stalls who turns to her and catches her eye, opening his eyes wide and putting a finger to his pursed lips. She realizes with a shock it is her younger boy, Phillip, her pet, who has dared to turn and glare at her with something like horror in his gray-green eyes to tell her to sing more softly. He turns to face forward toward the altar and to whisper something to the boy at his side who grins.

Then they all have to sit down, and the thin, gray-haired headmaster climbs the steps shakily to the blond wooden pulpit to give the sermon. His reedy voice rises and falls monotonously, saying something long and dreary about God of the Rushing Wind or Water and the beauty of the heavenly mountains which Bill thinks is a lot of nonsense. What a waste of her boys' time, when they could be out in the fresh air in the real garden having fun with her.

She has never liked the oppressive atmosphere in this chapel. It makes her think again of her death, of loss, of all the sadness and suffering in the world. The Church, despite all its good intentions, has often done much harm, over the years, dividing people and pitting them one against another, making war, not peace.

Truthfully, she has never liked to go to church, which is why she rarely comes to visit the school. In fact, she has never had much time for religious people, who often appear hypocritical to her, using their religion as a club to bludgeon others into doing what they want them to do. She does not like their singing to God and praying to be good, to love their neighbors, while for the most part ignoring all the poverty and suffering around them.

At this school, one of the best in the town, she knows the boys have to attend chapel daily. Her boys have been here from an early age, first as day boys and then as boarders, and indeed, seem very happy in the company of these teachers, mostly young idealistic bachelors from England who know little about life in South Africa or perhaps, life anywhere. Apparently, unlike their mother, who skipped school as much as she could, her boys actually enjoy reading dry books, learning poetry by heart, doing mathematics, where they shine particularly—"Algebra is interesting, Mother: you look for the unknown, the X, you see"—and all the dull dates of world history. They even enjoy writing essays. They are always reading or scribbling away. "Go outside and get some fresh air," she tells them. "Go and have some fun."

"This is fun," they say, blinking at her, looking up from their books like moles emerging into the light. It seems to her that they live much of their lives in an unreal world, and that anything they have learned about life comes from a book.

She is relieved when the service is finally over and the doors are thrown open, and the boys file out down the aisle and into the lengthening shadows and cooler air of the scented garden. She waves to them wildly as they go past her, but they do not seem to see her, and she pushes her way through the crowd to find them outside, burdened with her basket which, like her past, feels increasingly heavy.

She catches up to them, standing in a clot of boys under

a syringa tree. She puts down her basket and hugs them and kisses them enthusiastically, saying, "I have missed you so much!" in a loud voice. They stare down at her with cool expressions, rubbing her lipstick from their chiseled cheeks, as though they are not quite sure who she is.

How beautiful they are, she thinks with a tilt of the heart—almost unbearably so, anonymously, with their smooth alabaster skin, their misty gray-green eyes, their perfect profiles. They seem almost unreal to her: too neat, too clean, too quiet for adolescent boys. They look stiff and a little embarrassed and almost invisible in the fading light in their Sunday white shirts now that they have taken off their jackets. White on white.

"Are you feeling alright? You look a little anemic," she says, anxiously peering at Phillip, who just scowls rather rudely and shrugs and says, "I'm *fine,* Mother."

She thinks sadly how little they look like her side of the family. All her family have glossy dark hair, large, dark eyes, and dusky skin which turns a golden brown in the sun. All her family are small with tiny hands and feet. She thinks suddenly, as they stand in awkward silence by her side in the shadows, that they could almost belong to someone else. They look much more like her dead husband's side of the family, particularly the older one, who at seventeen is already tall, well over six foot, and so slim, with endless legs, long, strong arms, long tapering fingers and long feet. Despite his height he has remained narrow-chested and narrow-hipped, and when he gives a rare smile, shows his fine, white teeth. He looks a little like a Thoroughbred horse. Indeed he likes to ride and keeps his own filly at the school. How earnest they both look, she cannot help thinking, with her husband's coloring: the strawberry blond hair, the pale skin that does not take the sun. They are his boys through and through: hardworking, well-meaning, intellectual snobs. She's not quite sure what to say to them anymore.

As she looks at them in the fading evening light and long shadows, they look old to her, despite their fresh skin and hair. She sees them as strangers, someone else's children, the kind of people she would never feel at ease with: tall and straight-backed, they have maroon pins on their white shirts for good deportment, and an array of other badges for merit, well-intentioned people—scientists, mathematicians, missionaries, schoolteachers, perhaps even revolutionaries—she's always afraid they will end up in jail for their political views, encouraged by their teachers here—social workers or even writers of learned and earnest books like those she fears. Not the sort of people who would know how to enjoy a lot of money, surely. What would they do with it? Give it away to some religious charity or radical cause?

Phillip whispers in her ear, "You know you don't have to wear a *hat* to chapel, Mother. None of the other mothers wears hats." She puts her hand protectively to the wide brim of her lovely mauve hat with all the many-colored flowers that Gladys had angled perfectly for her. What purpose would church serve if one couldn't even wear a hat? she would like to say. He looks down at her pink, high-heeled Italian shoes she spent a fortune on, and she can see her son is embarrassed by her elegance. Indeed, she stands out. She surveys the other hatless, gloveless mothers in their dull, shabby clothes, their sensible shoes. They seem to stare disapprovingly at her. She feels overdressed and out of place. She should never have come. No one else is wearing even a string of pearls let alone three with a sapphire clasp. There is a woman in dusty jodhpurs and a rather dirty blouse who looks as though she must have just got off her horse! Bill overhears her say, "Does that woman think she's going to tea with the Queen?" surely referring to her. Bill gives her a dirty look. How can a woman come to Sunday chapel in such attire, when she and Gladys have gone to so much trouble to make her sons proud. Still, perhaps she should have chosen a hat with a few less flowers.

Her boys do not even appreciate jewels. Perhaps she should leave them to her sisters, who adore them?

Phillip turns toward her, his eyes bright, speaking of the teacher she spotted in church, "Mr. Milne gave me an A for my essay on a mathematical revolution."

"Oh, good for you, darling," Bill replies, not quite sure how mathematics can be revolutionary but worried by the word *revolution*.

She disapproves of the humiliating laws of this country, the passes which the black people have to carry, the absurdly segregated beaches and benches, the ridiculous censoring of books. She believes Brazil solved the "color problem" by mixing the races, but she doesn't want to see her boys in jail. She's afraid these naive teachers are not aware of the danger of all this talk.

Phillip's report cards are ominously excellent, filled with phrases such as: "He always tries so very hard," which makes her want to weep at the thought of him straining his beautiful eyes and mind over his books. She would find indolent brilliance less disturbing. This excess of diligence has always worried her. She has warned her sons not to be too clever for their own good.

She is not sure that men who appear too clever, who know too many threatening facts or hold too many firm opinions on the state of the world, do very well in life. In her experience, what men in power want from others is to be made to feel brilliant. They want charming young men who ask them what *they* think, and who admire them. Too many degrees or even too many opinions might hinder her boys' chances in life, rather than enhance them. Also, she has the suspicion that clever people have more psychological problems.

There is an awkward silence.

"You remember my best friend, Mother?" her older boy, Mark, asks, gesturing politely to the boy who stands close at his side in silence, a plain boy who has acne, wears thick glasses and heavy lace-up shoes, and looks serious.

"Of course, I do. Lovely to see you, Joseph," she says, and gives him a big hug. His name is Joseph, isn't it?

Mark says the boy's name is Travis. She feels like a fool. Things are not going as planned. She opens up the basket she has placed at the base of the tree and takes out the chicken, which looks even bigger, shimmering in its silver paper. She holds it aloft triumphantly as her servant did, and asks if they are hungry. A little gravy leaks from the paper and trickles down into her pink gloves and onto the ground. The boys look around furtively at the other mothers and the teachers, and Mark whispers that the parents are not supposed to bring food for their children after chapel, that they'll all get into trouble. "You know that, Mother, don't you?" he says, and puts the chicken quickly back in the basket.

"And do you always do what you are told? How will you ever have any fun, any joy?" she says with a little grin. Really, what milquetoasts! How will they survive in life? She feels the terror and hurt in her life came when she allowed her family to penetrate her wall of protection, to be the authors of her story.

"I try very hard to do what I'm supposed to do," Mark says sanctimoniously, and puts a hand on the lid of the basket to push it farther down.

She lies, telling them the Zulu cooked the chicken especially for them. She will say anything that seems necessary. At his name, both her boys turn sad. "Tell him I miss him so much," Phillip says, and she feels a pang of jealousy. They feel closer to him than to her. They have always adored him, learned his language, and spent their afternoons listening to him at the bottom of the garden tell stories of the many battles and victories of his people.

"We could go to the bottom of the garden here, and no one would see," she suggests now, widening her eyes at them. They look down at her with disapproval.

A bell rings, and they announce they have to go to supper. They say good-bye and rush off quickly in the pearly dusk with a brief, cool kiss on the cheek, sending their love and thanks once more to the old servant. She feels their relief at having an excuse to escape, and she, too, guiltily, is relieved to see them go.

She walks hurriedly across the tarred parking lot to the chauffeur, who lounges against the side of the car, talking with someone, and waiting for her in the lengthening shadows. The stars are visible in a midnight blue sky when she jumps into her pink Cadillac, alone in the back, slamming the door and telling him for the second time to step on it. She pulls off her stained gloves and devours the chicken herself, tearing at the plump flesh of a thigh with her bare fingers. She even pops a potato into her mouth as they go out through the gates. She passes the chauffeur a drumstick and urges him to eat, too, but not to let the cook know who enjoyed the food. She says, "He'd kill me, if he knew I'd eaten the *n'kosasaan*'s chicken."

As she arrives at the door of her flat, she remembers her first sight of her aunts' house, that evening, more than thirty years ago in Kimberley. She recalls standing in front of the door, holding Isaac's hand. They looked at one another and almost turned and left. If only they had done so.

CHAPTER EIGHT

1925

BILL HAD SUGGESTED KIMBERLEY, IN THE NORTHERN CAPE, because of its distance from Johannesburg. She remembered her aunts' house as one with many rooms and the sound of the municipal water wagons, which passed at dawn to settle the dust, and woke her.

Bill's father had attended the Kimberley high school as a boy, and his sisters had attended the school for girls. It was here that he had walked past the monument commissioned by Rhodes to those who had died during the siege by the Boers. He himself had hidden in a dugout with his mother and sisters. He told Bill the story of watching a native woman, carrying a bundle on her head, walking down the street, the shock of seeing her hit by a shell, her head and the bundle falling to the ground. It was here, too, that Bill's father had joined de Beers, as her grandfather had done before him. Her grandfather had dug in the Big Hole and learned about diamonds in the place where so many had been found, so many fortunes made and lost.

She had thought Kimberley would be a good place for both of them, with her three maiden aunts still there, living in the family's old house on a narrow plot of land, bought by her grandfather in a moment of prosperity, after the sale of a diamond claim. She had thought she and Isaac could find refuge here, and that surely there would be many possibilities of work for him, though her father had told her that it was not what it had once been, the diamond mines no longer being worked as they once had, and that it had become in some ways an ironic monument to the past.

She had calculated that the three maiden women would have pity on them, take them in, keep their secret, at least for a while until Isaac got himself settled. She had thought that, having been deprived themselves of men in their lives because of their father's cruel will, her aunts would understand and condone this sudden love and youthful passion, sharing it vicariously.

They had, indeed, welcomed the dusty, tired couple with enthusiasm, "Goodness, how you have grown, darling child!" "What a beautiful young lady, our favorite niece!" "What a lovely surprise!" the aunts exclaimed all speaking at once, fluttering around her excitedly, pecking at her cheeks, stroking her hands and hair like three hungry birds. At first, she could hardly distinguish one from the other: they all seemed similarly white-plumed, erect, and slim.

"This is Isaac," Bill said, smiling up at him proudly. The aunts looked up at him curiously in their pale, old-fashioned, high-collared dresses and their odor of camphor and 4711 eau de cologne, all crowded together in the narrow, dark entrance hall with its hat stand shaped like a leafless tree.

Their immediate concern was with the dust. They wanted them to bathe. "I'll run a bath for you, Bill!" said Aunt Winnie, the youngest, a slim woman in her late forties, who still had traces of red in her white hair. But Bill protested, saying they were hungry and thirsty, and wanted to eat first.

"You must be exhausted. What a long voyage! In an open car! Good heavens, child! What were you thinking?" they exclaimed, having observed their arrival through the window.

They had sent the couple off together into the small dark cloakroom to wash up while they assembled a meal. As Bill stood with Isaac before the mirror over the basin with the musty odor of raincoats, boots, straw gardening hats, and mud-caked gloves hanging from pegs on the walls, she caught a glimpse of their faces side by side, his narrow, intelligent one beside the soft oval of her own. He turned to smile at her, love and trust in his dark eyes. Faintly, in the corridor outside, she could hear the aunts chattering away excitedly. "Do you think Robert knows they are here?"

When the couple emerged, Aunt May, the middle one, who was the plumpest of the three, in her pink dress, her hair short and curly, ushered them into the dining room with its square table, cream crocheted tablecloth, and the French windows which opened onto the small garden at the back. They had Gladys bring out everything she had in the kitchen, giving the appearance of a feast. Spread before them was an assortment of food: cold chicken, ham, and scrambled eggs with tomatoes and parsley just plucked from the garden, pickles, bread pudding with cream, ripe apricots, and plums.

There was even a bottle of sherry and some tiny cut glasses, which must have been taken down from a high shelf and dusted off for the occasion. The aunts clucked over the couple sympathetically.

Having eaten as much as she could, Bill paused. Her heart beat so hard she felt the table, with all its pale pink platters, its remnants of the feast, the tomatoes bleeding into the ham, would shake. She stammered that they had something they wanted to ask. They needed help. There was a silence as all three aunts looked worriedly and furtively from Bill to Isaac. Then Bill asked if they would consent to come the next day and be their witnesses at the civil ceremony. The aunts stared, their mouths open in a sudden, awkward silence.

Bill looked anxiously from one to the next, as each of the three averted her gaze. Finally, Aunt Maud, the eldest, in her fifties, the hair that framed her face piled high on her head in a bun and already quite white, glanced at her sisters, trouble in her dark brown eyes. "Isn't this a bit hasty?" she said, looking at Isaac, who was finishing off his chicken and wiping a piece of brown bread around his plate with gusto.

Aunt May fiddled with the cameo at the neck of her dress and said to Bill, "You have all the time in the world! Seventeen! Bless my heart!"

Aunt Winnie, the youngest, fear in her watery brown eyes, said, "What did your father say? I'm afraid he would not approve. You know what he's like, a stickler for form. I don't think he can give you his blessing. He would want a church wedding, a white dress, all of that sort of thing, don't you think?"

"A church wedding would not be possible, as I am Jewish," Isaac explained matter-of-factly.

"That's why we came to you," Bill replied, smiling at her aunts. "We hoped you would help us."

"But you are both so very young," Aunt May reiterated, shaking her short curls, perspiration on her brow, her cheeks flushed with the rare glass of sherry. She pressed her hands together in a position of prayer and added, "Surely this could wait for a while?"

After the dessert, which they ate in silence, the couple rose quickly to help carry the dishes into the kitchen. "One witness ought to do for us," Isaac whispered to Bill and indicated Gladys, raising his eyebrows at her back.

The dignified lady who had been with the family since Bill's father was born and who lived in the house with the aunts was washing the dishes, her back to them, bent over the sink. Bill stood beside her and put her hand around her waist, her head on her shoulder. She asked her in a whisper, "You will go with us to get married, won't you, Gladys?" Gladys did not reply but looked down at Bill and took Isaac's empty plate.

She shook her head in disapproval and whispered, "It will bring trouble."

"We need you, so we can get married," Bill said.

Then Gladys looked at her from the corner of her eye, shrugged her shoulders, pursed her lips, and nodded her head, sighing. It was the only encouragement they received.

The aunts ushered Bill into the big bathroom, Winnie turning on the taps hard for her, pouring the bath salts which fell like ashes through the air into the old tub with its animal paws for feet. "Think this over carefully," she told Bill as she closed the door on her. Then Bill undressed and sank down into the hot water. She scrubbed carefully between her legs, which she had not been able to do in the hotel. After they had both bathed, the aunts led them firmly to separate rooms at opposite ends of the corridor.

CHAPTER NINE

※

1925

BEFORE DAWN, THEY BOTH ROSE SILENTLY. WHEN ISAAC KNOCKED softly on her door, Bill was already in the white cotton dress she had made with the silk snood in her dark hair. She had picked a bunch of daisies from the garden which she held in her trembling hands. They found Gladys in the kitchen, waiting for them, two cups of black coffee ready.

They climbed into the car, and Isaac struggled to start the engine. It turned over, and as he put his foot on the accelerator, backing out of the driveway and swerving into the street, Bill saw Aunt Maud running out the front door, waving wildly, but too late. As the sun flamed the sky, the three of them took off, Gladys clutching her large handbag to her chest and making little gasping noises through her uneven teeth as Isaac careened along the street.

Gladys knew the way to the magistrate's court with its elaborate crenellated clock tower rising over the city. The sun shone down on them from a pale sky, a warning of heat up ahead. Only a few motorcars, trolley buses, and a donkey's cart, a few silent black and white figures were in the streets at this hour.

Despite their early arrival, they were kept waiting. They sat along the wall in the corridor, the three of them in silence. No one seemed in a hurry. They were finally ushered inside by the magistrate, a large bald gentleman in a dark suit and dark waistcoat, his gold fob watch on his chest. He told the couple to sit down and glanced at Gladys. "This . . . person is your witness?" he asked, raising his eyebrows at the couple when they were seated before him, ready to sign their names.

"As good a witness as anyone else, I suppose," Isaac dared to say. The magistrate looked up at Gladys standing there, solemn and dignified in her dark dress, cream hat, and gloves. He asked her if she could sign her name. The couple looked up at her hopefully, and she nodded her head firmly, making the flowers in her hat shake at the brim. She bent down to write slowly and painfully, each letter a work of art: *Gladys Browning* in a shaky hand.

Afterward, Isaac said, "Come on, I'm taking you both out to lunch."

"Let's go to the Ritz," Bill suggested, naming a place she remembered from special birthdays and other celebrations. The couple was ushered into the high-ceilinged room with its white-jacketed waiters, its red carpet, and the potted palms, though Gladys was told she would have to wait in the car. Recklessly, Isaac ordered a bottle of champagne, spending all of the money that remained on the three-course meal with thick cream soup and roast beef with Yorkshire pudding followed by granadilla cake, which he had the waiters carry outside for all three of them to share, giggling with Gladys in the car.

Later, they sauntered slowly up the garden path in the October sunshine, somewhat inebriated, flushed and laughing at their success, followed by poor Gladys, who had eaten her piece of cake and drunk her glass of champagne and fallen fast asleep while waiting for them to finish their meal in the car.

Then Bill saw Aunt Winnie come running out of the front door, waving her hands warningly at the couple, coming down the flower-lined path, her long reddish hair floating wildly behind her, her apron strings untied.

Aunt Winnie stood before them and said, panting, clasping her hands, "They are here."

Isaac and Bill gazed at her blankly, and she explained, "Your parents."

"How did they know we were here?" Bill said, knowing the answer even as she asked the question.

"We thought it for the best. We didn't know what else to do. I have to warn you, they have taken it hard . . ."

How could she not have realized that would be her aunts' first response? Why had she not understood that their loyalty lay with their brother, whom they adored? Her parents had taken the night train and rushed down to find them.

Then she was aware of the lateness of the day, the dimming light, the deep midnight blue of the sky, the drooping spring flowers in the parched garden after the unusual heat of the day, the silence in the street.

Isaac looked at Bill, and she remembers now how she put the little bunch of daisies down on the round wicker table on the verandah so as not to have to walk inside with her bouquet in her hands. She had picked the flowers at dawn, and held them wilting during the brief ceremony in her trembling fingers, and kept them with her in the car reviving them in a glass of water.

CHAPTER TEN

⁂

1956

AS SHE CLIMBS OUT OF THE CAR IN THE GARAGE OF HER FLAT, SHE decides she'll dismiss her servant, have a bowl of soup and a glass of whiskey, and go to bed immediately; but unexpectedly, when she enters the lounge, she finds someone waiting for her. At first, standing with his back to her in the shadows of the pink light of her floor lamp, she's not sure who it is—a stranger whose presence alarms and yet thrills her. Whom has the cook allowed in? Who would come to see her at this hour? For a moment it occurs to her, her mind on Isaac, that it is someone from her past.

"Auntie, aren't you glad I came to see you?" he says, turning from the painting he has been studying to face her with indolent grace, smiling with apparent pleasure at the sight of her, coming toward her with a swaying step, both hands dramatically lifted toward her. He kisses her on both cheeks twice, as though he were on the stage in a French play. "You smell wonderful," he says. "Is it Chanel?"

It is not a mysterious stranger at all, but her older sister's nephew, Whit Johnson. He is indeed an actor, having studied drama at the Royal Academy of Dramatic Art in London. He has been waiting for her.

"I'm sorry to have kept you waiting," she says and calls for the cook, whom she now scolds, "Why didn't you bring out the tray with the drinks and something to eat, some nuts, some crackers, cheese? Turn on more lights."

"He's left you here all in the dark," she says to Whit as the cook bustles about, his starched uniform rustling, his face increasingly solemn with disapproval. He doesn't like her to drink, she knows, and particularly not with men.

"Is that a new painting?" Whit asks, gesturing toward the painting of a bay in the Cape by William Timlin that once hung in the lounge of the big house she sold after her husband's death. "It's lovely," he adds, and she feels he is complimenting her, which he proceeds to do. "Where have you been today, looking so beautiful, Aunt?" he adds.

"I made the mistake of going to see my children at Sunday chapel," she confides, and laughs and collapses into a chair and pushes off her sling-back shoes with her toes, tosses the hat onto the sofa. She needs a drink and feels the urge to joke about religion, her love for her children, her excessive devotion. "Ah children!" she says wryly, "We give our whole lives to them, and what do they give us back? I'm sure you were a devoted son, Whit, but honestly it's not often the case!" His mother died when he was quite young; she knows that he adored her and hates his father, a lawyer who has always disapproved of him and treated him severely and with incomprehension. She takes her whiskey-and-soda from the old cook's shaking hand and gulps greedily.

"You are too devoted to your children. You spend too much time worrying about their every little wish—isn't that true?" Whit says, taking his drink and including the servant in the conversation. The cook scowls at him darkly and says nothing, just turning his back. "But it is. They have everything in the world, lucky devils. They don't know how lucky they are to have such a wonderful mother, such an interesting woman," he says, looking at her askance, fluttering his long, dark eyelashes, pursing his lips, and ignoring the cook, who glares at him and leaves the room.

Whit goes on, "Really, we know so little about you, Auntie. Pie's always saying you could tell us a story or two. You should write a book about your life."

She wonders what Pie has dared to tell him. Surely she would not have confided in him? "What has Pie been telling you?" she asks nervously, fussing with her skirt. It occurs to her that he might know more than she would like.

"You should spend more time enjoying yourself, having fun," he says and sinks down gracefully onto her beige carpet with the pink flowers, at her feet, as if to demonstrate the art, holding the nape of his neck and throwing back his handsome head. He flashes a smile that makes a parenthesis of dimples appear around his well-formed mouth. "Such a beautiful woman and young, but not too young, Aunt! No one lives forever. You ought to take advantage of every moment. Seize the day!" he says and waves a hand gracefully around the pretty room. He looks strong and handsome and sleepy and from the way he reclines at her feet, lounging in her living room, from his easy attitude, she senses he feels as comfortable with her as she does with him. She has known him since he was a boy.

He looks as though he is dreaming of something pleasant. She remembers that her husband also liked this young man and found him intelligent, talented, and amusing, and had even helped pay for his acting studies in England. She remembers Whit as a boy bringing them a model of a theater he had made himself with great skill. He is very good with his hands, she thinks, and remembers other hands, the long adroit fingers sorting diamonds that day in her youth.

She smiles at him.

He says, "You must be lonely now, sometimes, Aunt."

The phrase *lonely as the moon* comes to her mind.

"Do you ever imagine falling in love again?" he asks.

She would not mind falling in love, or rather, having someone fall in love with her. She would like to have some handsome younger man like this one, at her side, devoted to her. She admires the way his thick hair gleams almost red in the rosy light. She likes what she thinks of as the sensitive sadness in his large dark eyes. She watches as he takes off his V-neck sweater and bunches it behind him to form a pillow on the floor. He says, "We've been rehearsing all day, and I'm exhausted," and yawns, and his eyelids droop sleepily, seductively, and his hair falls into his eyes. It touches her to think of him coming directly from his rehearsal to see her. He seems to her a most charming young man, still in his late twenties, with even features which he tilts up to the light a little theatrically, as though someone were taking his photograph in profile.

She is relieved to talk to someone who is no blood relation of hers, though he always calls her "Aunt," endearingly. He will, surely, ask nothing of her, not judge her, and avoid talk of revolution or mathematical matters.

He is pleasantly if informally dressed—she likes people to make a sartorial effort, which he has done for her, wearing cream linen pants, pleated at the waist, and a tight-fitting blue shirt of smooth, almost transparent stuff, though he has almost no money and will never make much.

He says, as though divining her thought, "I wish I were rich and could take you out somewhere wonderful for dinner—candlelight, champagne, caviar, that's what you deserve. I wish we could go dancing together under the stars." He makes an eloquent gesture of offering something with his fine, white, empty hands.

"You're a darling," she says and reaches out to clutch his hands, which are warm in hers. It occurs to her that he is exactly at an age when he might be her son, and the thought brings tears to her eyes.

She wonders what he would do if she opened her arms and begged him to come to her, to take her loneliness from her. She wants to stroke his hair, to nestle his head against her breasts, to let him comfort her. She would like someone with all the grace of a dancer beside her. She is convinced he is as good a dancer as she is. How she misses dancing! She imagines a sea voyage to Europe with a young man like him, someone gentle, courteous, and amusing who would make only filial demands on her. She sees herself dancing in a long blue net dress on the deck of a luxurious liner, the moon bright, the smell of the ocean in the air.

She has taken her own boys to Europe during the holidays, of course, but they came armed with lists from their teachers of places to visit and things to do. They wanted to tick off the items: the ancient churches, the great museums, the famous paintings, the ruined monuments. "I'm getting a bit tired of ruins," she would say during their stay in Rome, reclining in the sunlight on her bed at the Hassler. "You two go on your own to the Forum today, will you? I think I'll just stay in the room and relax."

"We have to see Raphael's *Madonna of the Pinks*," Phillip would say, looking worriedly at his list on a visit to London. What intellectual snobs they are, what painfully earnest creatures! How did she produce them? They wanted to read their fat, serious books: *War and Peace* and *Vanity Fair* and even something about *Great Contemporaries* by Winston Churchill, which she found Phillip reading one night under the blankets with a torch. She kept saying, as the train wound its way through the high mountains, fir trees, and snow of Switzerland—snow, they had never seen before, "Oh, look! Look! Do look at the scenery, boys, for goodness' sake! You can read your books at home!" but obviously they preferred words on a page, an idea in their heads, an ideal to be followed, to the reality of the beauty around them.

Now she sits back in her chair and says sadly, "There's a point when children aren't who they were anymore. They're just 'over there' somewhere—a couple of strangers."

"Really, one does wonder sometimes why people want so desperately to procreate," this only son adds pleasantly.

She would like his opinion on the matter of the money. She says, "I'm not sure what to do about my boys, how much to help them on their way. Mr. Parks called this afternoon. He wants me to make a will. I know he expects me to leave the money to the boys, but it's such a difficult decision," she says.

He considers and says, "It might be better for them to have to make their own way in life. If you don't, it tends to do things to you. It's important to want something, isn't it?"

"Do you think so?" she says, and thinks how wise he is at such a young age. "And what do you want?" she asks him, looking into his soft, dark eyes.

"I would like to be able to devote myself entirely to my acting and not have to do what it takes to make ends meet," he says at once. "Money buys you time." She knows he is obliged to work as a waiter, and perhaps he even has to do other, more demeaning things?

They drink several whiskey-and-sodas together, and the cook comes in and out of the room in his silent, reproachful shoes, reluctantly replenishing their drinks, adding ice and soda. He has never liked men to come to the house since her husband's death and positively scared away an English lord who had courted her assiduously and probably had his eye on her fortune. He watches over her and her boys jealously, she thinks with amusement. She wonders if he even spreads chicken blood around in the garden to keep the evil spirits away from them. Yet he has become the man in their lives.

"Bring us some supper, will you?" she asks. "You must have something in the kitchen for us." It is Sunday night, and she knows she should have let him have the evening off. But what would he do with it? He would only lie in his room and smoke his pipe. When he goes on holiday he gets robbed on the train and comes back looking like a skeleton. She intends to let both the servants off tomorrow afternoon, anyway, after the luncheon for her family. He scowls at her and clatters around in the kitchen, which is just off the lounge and within earshot, but eventually he brings them each a bowl of delicious-smelling tomato soup with crisp croutons in a silver bowl on a tray. He stands there stolidly, looking stubborn. He is apparently not going to set the table for dinner in the dining room.

"Oh, alright, just serve us here, then," she says, and they eat informally on white linen napkins on their laps, facing one another on the chintz-covered sofa before the empty fireplace. When they have finished and the cook has taken the bowls, she tells him to leave the dishes and go to bed. It is late. But he shakes his head and says he will wait to lock up the flat. "A lot of *skelms* around," he mutters darkly, looking at poor Whit.

"Suit yourself," Bill says, and shrugs and listens to him crashing the dishes around in the sink, rather like her conscience. She turns to Whit, "Tell me something amusing—I don't want to think about that dreadful chapel service—all that awful praying and hymn singing. There are so many things I don't want to think about," she says, and puts her hands to her head where there is a buzzing noise.

"Shall I tell you the plot of something I'm reading?" he asks. "I'm reading such a good novel by . . ."

She raises a hand. "No, no, all those thick novels you and my boys want me to read are too sad. I don't want to hear about unhappiness and poor people in prison, all that weeping and moaning and gnashing of the teeth, all those poor suffering souls. I can't do anything for them. I've had too much unhappiness in my own life to want to read about it," she says, and waves away the ghosts of sorrow. "Do the play you're rehearsing, will you?" She's seen the thriller in London, though she can no longer remember what it's called. Nor does she remember who does the murder except that it is no one you would suspect.

He rises obligingly and acts out the plot, performing each scene in detail, all the many different roles, his voice and his demeanor changing dramatically, going from a high falsetto to a deep bass, throwing himself into attitudes, clasping his hands with fervor before him and clutching his head as though it might explode with despair. She laughs, enthralled by the dramatization, seeing herself in the role of the beautiful, rich woman who is killed for her fortune. Everyone seems to have a secret to hide, and thus everyone is equally culpable.

He bows low at the end, and she claps loudly. They both drink several more glasses of the excellent red wine they have had with their soup. Then he takes his leave of her, kissing her on both cheeks again twice and saying with great sincerity, slurring his words, "Aunt, you are *fundamentally* a good woman."

She laughs and says, "Come back soon, will you. I am happy near you. You have cheered me up, after all those ridiculous hymns." He sings a few verses of "Abide with Me," as though it were a romantic song in a musical. He does a little jig in the hall, and says, "Of course I will. It's always a pleasure to make you happy—and remember, take a lover, lots of them!" There is an expression of such tender devotion in his brown eyes. Though he has no claim on her, though he has confided in her that he will never marry and lives in a dreadful small dark flat, she suddenly wonders if she should really invite him to go on a tour with her. What a wonderful companion he would be! What *fun* they would have! What if she left him her money! It seems a brilliant idea. What would Mr. Parks have to say about that? It would give him pause. It would be an action of merit. Actors, even good ones, rarely make money, and he would know how to enjoy hers.

"Really, Auntie, a different one for each day of the week!" he reiterates.

She sighs and thinks she does not want all the grief of even one lover anymore. Passion, she knows all too well, brings in its wake too much pain. Besides, at her age, whom would she find? "What would I want with some old boy?" she says.

"Why would it have to be an *old* boy—why not a *young* one?" he says flirtatiously, staring into her eyes.

She laughs but wonders why he is telling her this. What has he been told about the lover from her past?

As she lets him kiss her good-bye on her cheek in the hall, she smells the sweet scent of his smooth skin. She presses his hand as she opens the door on the scented night garden, the honeysuckle and verbena that grows around her door, and she remembers her awful arrival with Isaac on her aunts' doorstep in Kimberley, after their wedding.

CHAPTER ELEVEN

✵

1925

WHEN THEY ENTERED THE OLD HOUSE AND STOOD TOGETHER IN the dark hall staring down the shotgun passage, they could already hear her mother's pathetic wails. She clutched Isaac's hand, appalled. It sounded as if someone had died. They looked at each other, widened their eyes, gripped hands harder and hesitated, contemplating escape, but they had nowhere to go. They entered the lounge, finding her mother and father there, with the dusty proteas in a bowl and the canister of stale mints on the round mahogany table in the middle of the room, with its smell of camphor and cloves.

Her father stood solemnly by the mantel, fingering his stiff, bristly mustache, drawing himself up as if he could increase his height, while her mother sat, a picture of woe, bent over in an armchair in the shadows, her shoulders shaking, a handkerchief to her eyes, her long, thick, graying hair loose and untidy around her shoulders and face, her clothes disheveled, her stockings rolled down her ankles.

"After all I have suffered," she kept saying while her

sisters-in-law fussed around her, offering mint tea, and smelling salts, suggesting she lie down. She had managed to capture everyone's attention, to turn the room into a clinic. When she lifted her face up to the couple, it was pathetically red and swollen from weeping through the night. She was undone, Bill could see, and despite herself, her heart tilted with sympathy. "How could you do this to me?" her mother exclaimed the moment she saw them and wept loudly and clasped her hands together dramatically.

Her father told them to sit down. She sat on the stiff horsehair sofa while Isaac stood stalwartly at her side, his hand on her shoulder to steady her. He lifted his chin bravely and announced that they were now man and wife. They had signed the papers in the magistrate's office.

Her father, not a tall man, and usually somewhat stooped from staring at gemstones, surged up and down with short nervous steps, thrusting back his shoulders, waving his hands in the air, and saying "That's nonsense, my boy. Balderdash!"

"But we are married. A magistrate married us. Tell him, Bill," Isaac reiterated, looking at her father with amazement. "Where is Gladys? She was our witness. She signed the paper, too," he added, but Gladys had disappeared to the kitchen and was probably listening through the door.

"Gladys, a witness to a marriage! What rubbish!" her father said. Isaac stared at him in disbelief. Clearly he had never imagined such opposition, a denial of the simple facts, a legal document. Isaac was a believer in the Law, a man of the Book.

"Yes, we are married," she said, but her voice faltered, and indeed, it now seemed less credible to her, already almost a dream. She was on the point of tears, to have caused this unhappiness.

Her father said that, in the eyes of his family, this was not a proper marriage. "Marriage," he said, "is a Christian ceremony where a man and a woman come to church, accompanied by their families to swear their fidelity and love before the eyes of the community, and before God."

Isaac said angrily, "You are suggesting that people who are not Christians cannot marry? That my parents are living in sin!"

Bill's father told him to stop shouting. He said that from whatever religion you happened to be, his daughter was not of age, and therefore needed parental consent to marry. Isaac had acted unlawfully. It could and would have to be annulled. "It will not stand in a court of law; on the contrary, you could be punished for this," he said.

"Don't you want me to be happy?" she asked her father, turning to him, beseeching him, tears trickling down her cheeks, trying to speak to him without words, pressing her hands together in prayer.

"It's because I do, that I cannot allow you to ruin your life. I'm only doing what is best for you," he said to her, coming over and taking both her hands gently in his.

"You are ruining my life," Bill said, weeping, hanging her head.

"We will not discuss this any further. Neither of you is old enough to understand the gravity and consequences of your act," her father said solemnly.

He turned to Isaac, his voice gaining in strength, speed, and force. "I must ask you to leave this house, immediately.

Believe me, I have nothing against the Jewish people, indeed I admire them, and I have regarded you as a colleague, but you have taken advantage of me to steal the most precious thing I possess. You are now no longer welcome in my home or the home of anyone in my family!"

Isaac looked at him and then down at Bill, squeezed her shoulder, and said, "Come on Bill. They cannot force you to stay here. They cannot separate us. Come with me."

Bill's mother said, sobbing loudly, "I don't care about myself and what you do to me but don't hurt my children. I only care about my children. They are my body and soul. If you cannot think of the shame this will bring on me and your father, think of your sisters' lives. Think of what this will do to them. Think of what this scandal will do to your darling little brother's prospects, if you go off with this man. Who will marry them?" her mother wept. "Ruined! Ruined! And your father not a healthy man, you know that. His heart is not strong. He has worked himself to the death for all of you. This will finish him off. It will kill him: your folly, and your selfishness. You want to do that?" She turned to Isaac, and with hate blazing in her dark eyes, asked him, "Why have you done this to us?"

Isaac took Bill by the hand. "Don't listen to them. We've done nothing wrong. Come with me. We'll go to my family." Bill rose to her feet, walked a step beside him, wondering how they would get back to Johannesburg without any money and if his family would indeed take them in. Would they want to take her on, a Christian girl, not yet eighteen, with no money and no prospects?

Her father followed them. He put his hand on her arm,

and turned her to face him. He said, looking at her with tears in his brown eyes, "My darling girl, if you go off with this man, you understand, you will never see us again, none of us who love you so much. You will be dead to us. You'll be entirely on your own with foreigners, who eat gefilte fish and don't know the Lord's Prayer."

Bill stood before him, breathing hard, tears running down her cheeks. "Don't say that, please," she said.

Her father put his hands on her shoulders, his fingers digging into her flesh. "I will say it, and I mean it: for your own good, you must stay here where you belong, with your own flesh and blood. Isaac's family will not want you with them. How will you live? Trust me on this, my darling. You must stay with your aunts until the scandal has died down and then you can come back to us, your own family. We'll never speak of this again. We will forgive you and Isaac. We are Christian people who want the best for both of you. Think of Isaac, too. He is too young to take on the burden of a wife. You know that is right. You must let him go back to his people where he belongs and you must stay here." Tears fell down her cheeks as her father encircled her, held on to her tightly, pressed her head against his shoulder. Unable to move, unable to breathe, overcome with a wave of nausea, her knees weak, she leaned against him as she watched Isaac.

He stood for a moment, looking into her eyes, waiting. He said, "You are not going to listen to this?" Then he turned from her and walked to the door, swiveled on his heels to glance around the room, taking in the dusty pink proteas, the three maiden aunts hovering tremulously in the corner, her weeping mother, her father, and her, with a look

of hatred in his dark eyes. He regarded them all with disbelief and disgust.

"I can't believe you people," he said drawing himself up
with disdain. He looked back at Bill as she tried to move out
of her father's arms, but she could see she had lost him, his
green eyes filled with rage at her betrayal. Her father held on
to her tightly, fiercely, while Isaac turned his back on her,
on all of them, and stalked out of the room. She listened to
his harsh, hard footsteps as he strode along the corridor to
collect his things, slammed the front door, started up the
motor of the blue Chevrolet. She ran to the door to go out
after him, but her father locked it, and her aunts crowded
around her and blocked her way. She could only beat her
hands against the wood. Where would he go? Would he
come back for her? Would she ever see him again?

PART TWO

CHAPTER TWELVE

1956

BILL IS AWAKENED ON MONDAY MORNING BY THE SOUND OF her two sisters calling out excitedly, "Bill! Bill! We're here!" She rises hastily from her bed and runs to the top of the stairs and hangs over the banister to watch. At the sight of her sisters in the hall, with their bright dresses and frivolous high-heeled shoes, their thin ankles and tiny, flapping hands, doing the Charleston on the parquet floor, singing "If you knew Susie like I knew Susie, Oh, oh, oh, what a girl!" she feels light-hearted again. She laughs and claps her hands and feels a great desire for mischief. She wants to talk without ceasing, to play the fool, to laugh.

She feels the sort of joy she felt as a child when her sisters would come back from school and she could come out of hiding from the bamboo at the bottom of the garden where she went to avoid classes, spending the day playing marbles in the dirt with the son of her mother's slatternly servant. She feels carefree and liberated as she watches them pirouette on the parquet floor, dressed as they were as teenagers in the twenties, with low waists and long beads, their hair shingled, short, and curly.

She comes tripping gaily down the stairs, half-dressed, without her tight corsets or stockings, and her sisters kiss her and tell her she looks well and beautiful, and she believes it. They sit together as they would do in the house on R Street on the screened-in verandah, gossiping, knitting, sewing, and sipping tea.

There are the cheerful chink of cups, the slurping of tea, the smell of freshly baked raisin scones the servant brings out, though her sisters have eaten breakfast. She feels hungry. She has eaten nothing since her bowl of soup last night with Whit, and she devours several scones and thanks the cook and says they are delicious as usual and looks about her, contentedly.

She is always afraid her sisters will think her money has made her grow proud, once only a blackbird like them but now in peacock's feathers. Yet, in some ways she has always been the star. She remembers how she would play "Simple Simon," jumping up and down on the lawn, her brother and sisters copying her.

Mostly, though, the women like to talk. There is no one whose conversation she finds quite as amusing. Neither of them has read much or even has anything original or witty to say. The subject that comes up most is dieting. They have many ideas on how to do it and periodically try one of their drastic diets, drinking nothing but buttermilk for several days or eating hard boiled eggs and steak or simply going to bed, fasting, and taking laxatives until they have lost five pounds. Sometimes, when she looks back on her life, she thinks of it as a series of periods of semi-starvation, alternating with periods of gluttony.

There is something so comforting about her sisters' frank conversation, the words themselves, the common childhood expressions, that delights her. They like and dislike the same people, have had many of the same experiences, and, above all, they know her past secrets, and though they never speak of them, there is no need to pretend, no fear of discovery or disapproval.

Pie, the eldest, who has remained slim in her early fifties, her dark hair short and permed into tight curls, says, "It's thanks to you, Bill, that we all get to be together like this every day and have such a good time. Without you we'd all have to go out to be governesses or something ghastly like that," shuddering at the thought of such an unlikely possibility and finishing off her cup of tea and asking for another one. She wears a brass bracelet on one arm to guard against rheumatism and a cream ribbon-knit cardigan Bill bought her. She says, "Poor Ted," speaking of her husband, "has gone and lost more money on the stock market. He says we're going to have to sell the blue Caddy that you gave us," referring to the Cadillac Bill's husband had given Pie's before he died.

"Don't worry, I'll buy you a new one," Bill says, but wonders where her elder sister is going with this.

Still, she cannot imagine her sisters as governesses or anything useful. Nothing they do has ever been. Their hands are always busy—they knit odd garments such as the swimming suits they made and embroidered with their initials for her boys which looked awful and stretched when they went into the pool and could not be worn again; they crochet light, pretty summer blankets; or do *petit point*, making cushions she does not really need and bright beaded handbags, in different colors, or they lay out patterns for their many low-cut, tight, pleated or frilled dresses, pinning them to the multicolored material on the shiny, smooth mahogany dining room table, holding steel pins in their mouths, then cut out the dresses with their pinking shears, which make a loud crunching noise and scar the mahogany dining room table below, much to the cook's displeasure.

Haze, the youngest sister, sighs and says, "You are so lucky that you found such a clever husband, one who made so much money." She has dark hair on her upper lip, as they all do, which they remove from time to time with hot wax. She has always been considered the brainy one, the shrewd one, who once worked as a secretary, and was in love with the married man for whom she worked. She knows how to add without using her fingers and to spell, which Bill does not, though Bill has learned, along the way, to quote some poetry: "If music be the food of love, play on," or, "Shall I compare thee to a summer's day?" or, dramatically, drawing herself up, "Break, break, break, on thy cold gray stones, oh sea! And I would that my tongue could utter, the thoughts that arise in me."

"He had more energy than a horse," Haze says, referring to Bill's husband, and finishing off her scone. "I can't believe he is dead."

Bill says truthfully, "What would I do without you?" and cannot resist confiding in them, though she hasn't meant to. "But I do worry. Mr. Parks called yesterday, asking me to make a will. He must think I'm about to die." Her sisters look at one another with a knowing, sideways look, and she suspects they have discussed their interest in this issue, as well as the possibility of her death.

She pauses for a moment as the cook collects the cups and the plates, and then says, "I don't know that my boys can really use the money. What would they do with it?"

Both nod their heads in agreement, their eyes glistening, listening attentively. Pie says, "Such good, modest boys who work so hard at school—not like us. None of us did that, did we?"

"Yes, yes, always playing chess," Haze agrees. "But we did work hard on other things, didn't we? All those alterations we did, for years and years. Sitting up all night sewing away to finish dresses! Do you remember? Certainly you have earned the right to live luxuriously, to have a good time," she says, and finishes off her scone.

"Actually, I was thinking of leaving it all to Whit," Bill says, to put a stop to this line of thinking. Her sisters stare at her and she realizes she rather enjoys the rapt attention the subject receives. She is aware this will cause consternation, though she doesn't expect her sisters' reaction.

Haze and Pie open their eyes and mouths wide. Together they shout out "Whit!" and clap their hands like actors in a Shakespearean play. They burst out laughing, doubling over with hilarity and reddened faces as though she has made a hilarious joke. "Of all people in the world! Can you imagine him with all that money? He'd spend it in a minute!"

She attempts to conjure up the initial rightness of her

decision, her feeling of tenderness for the young man, his devotion.

Haze adds, "He'd give it all to his boyfriend—what's the name of that fairy he lives with in Hillbrow, who dyes his hair yellow. Montague?"

Pie says, "Did he stop by last night? Maybe he was wondering the same thing as Parks and dragged himself from Montague's arms to come and see you."

Bill shuts her eyes for a moment on her sisters, the folly of her vision of waltzing with Whit under the stars coming to an end. She wonders if that, rather than the effort of a rehearsal, was why Whit seemed so exhausted. Did actors really rehearse on Sunday afternoons?

"Perhaps I shouldn't bother to make a will at all," she says crossly, getting up and lighting a cigarette, though she knows they give her a cough, blowing out the smoke and walking across the verandah. "I don't understand why Parks is so worked up about it. I'm not going to die tomorrow, you know."

"Of course not—but you can't be too careful." Pie trots out one of her favorite sayings but this time with a particularly knowing undertone and she adds, "particularly as you are on your own now and don't always take as good care of yourself as you might."

"What do you mean?"

"I just mean a woman alone is more vulnerable to, to, so many things," she says. Bill is not sure what she is referring to.

Haze says, "Certainly, I don't like you driving your own car at night, particularly after a party. You remember what happened with those poor boys in the back," referring to a slight scrape to her fender one evening, when she had driven herself and her boys home after dark.

"I rarely do that," Bill says, giving Haze an angry glare.

"And you have to watch out for men who could take advantage of you when you might be a little merry," Pie says, smiling. Who is she referring to? Whit? Mr. Parks, himself? Pie's son, Anthony, who is a poor scholar, steals money from her, sells cigarettes at school, and seems headed for a life of crime? Bill's past dealings with men? Certainly, though her sisters praise her deceased husband, they seem to have little faith in men. Pie cannot count on her husband, with his fine head of hair, to provide well for her or even to take care of the little he earns. He has an elderly mother who lives with them and keeps a dog called Willy which she expects him to walk at dawn. She is always coming into Pie's bedroom and saying, "Teddsy! Teddsy! Willy has to wee-wee!" and he rises from the conjugal bed obediently to do her bidding. Whenever Ted comes to her house he sits quietly against the wall with his fine, white hands folded in his lap.

Haze gave up her job as a secretary after her love affair and spent a period of mourning. As for their brother, though they all adore him, he is incapable of earning a living. He married a nurse who promptly gave up her career to bear several large, hungry babies.

Haze says, "Do you remember when we found that advertisement in the paper and told you to apply for the job?"

"I remember ironing my linen shirt and polishing my best shoes for your interview," Pie says. "It changed your whole life, that interview, didn't it?"

Bill says, "And yours, too."

Haze laughs and says, "I remember saying you'd only have to supervise. You certainly do that very well."

Bill scowls, but has to admit it is true. She has noticed that now, people often do what she wants them to do.

Haze says, "And I think I was the one who told you to tell Daddy you were going as a companion for the sick wife—and she did turn out to be well—sick—eventually, didn't she?"

Pie says, "I was the one who read the advertisement aloud, something like: *Experienced nurse-companion wanted for large house and garden in Hume Road, Dunkeld.* Was that it?"

Bill knew Dunkeld's huge houses, gardens, swimming pools, and tennis courts. It appealed to her. So did the salary.

"I was sure they'd give you the job. I was the one who telephoned for you. Do you remember?" Haze asks.

Bill thinks that it might have been wiser in the end if she had not gone to the interview at the house in Dunkeld.

CHAPTER THIRTEEN

1935

Haze was sitting close on Bill's left in her pink cotton dressing gown, eating a thick slice of bread and butter with jam, the newspaper before her, as her marmalade cat, Wurripumpkin, sat as usual on her lap. Charles was on Bill's right in his khaki shorts and long socks, dark hair slicked back, dreamily pushing a piece of bread around his plate of bacon and runny eggs, delaying his exit for work. Pie, who had been endlessly engaged to her solicitor, waiting for him to set the date, which his mother kept delaying with ailments of various kinds, sat somewhat primly, presiding at the top of the breakfast table, doling out the few extra slices of bread. Their father had already left for work and their mother was, as usual at that hour, still in bed.

Haze put her hand on Bill's arm and said, "Look at this. This would be perfect for you. Look how much they're paying, and it sounds so easy!" thrusting the newspaper before her.

In those days, she had decided that you only love once

in your life. She was not looking for love anymore. She had become restless and irritable. Above all she wanted to escape the crowded house, her sisters' endless reproaches, and her parents' silent disapproval. She wanted to travel the world, to go to what she thought of as "Gay Paris," to parties and to stand on the lawn in the blue light and sip champagne and throw back her head and laugh. She wanted to have a good time.

She always wanted her family to have a good time, too. She did not want her sisters to have to ruin their eyes sitting up late at night, doing alterations for difficult matrons, the way they all had been doing for years. She wanted Charles, ten years younger than she, to have a good time, too. He had, still has, a job with de Beers which their father had found for him, as he had never managed to pass his "matric." She has never been quite sure what Charles does there. When she asks him, he says he plays noughts and crosses. He was already running up bills for his father to pay.

She imagined her father might interpret the word "nurse-companion" as a domestic as he had the word "nurse" and say something like "No daughter of mine will hire herself out as a domestic," though he did not complain about the dressmaking they were obliged to do, sewing fine tucks until late at night, ruining their eyes, for what he called "pocket money," in order to make his own ends meet.

It was Haze who wrote down the telephone number on an edge of the newspaper and quietly tore it off. She smiled at her sisters over her shoulder and at Charles who looked at her inquiringly with his large dark eyes and thick lashes. She slipped into the passageway where the phone now hung on the wall and made the call in a loud voice. When she came back into the dining room, she announced, "She wants you there at two fifteen this afternoon."

"How did she sound?" Bill asked.

"A bit bizarre, almost as if she'd forgotten about the ad or never known about it. Perhaps the husband placed it. Hoity-toity accent. But she said you were the first to respond. So you'll be the first one she sees."

Bill hesitated, wondering why the woman sounded "bizarre" and what she was really expected to do. But she was not the sort of person to be put off easily.

Pie lent her a white linen blouse with a demure Peter-Pan collar, and sensible, narrow shoes which pinched her toes, and Haze, a narrow gray skirt with a wide black belt. They both brushed her curly hair till it glowed—she had always had good hair—and put a little scent behind her wrists and on her temples and even on the tip of her tongue, as though she might be going to kiss someone.

Haze made up a glowing reference for her and signed it with a titled name that was difficult to read. Lady Brentwood was the name they came up with after trying out more ridiculous ones like Lady Pomfret, or Lady Dinglebat, laughing together.

She never expected to be hired. It was part lark, part act of desperation, part attempt at restitution, the only way she could think of helping the family, of moving on. Besides, the whole family needed the money by then, with none of the three daughters married or gainfully employed apart from the sub rosa dressmaking, and their useless mother lounging on her bed eating bonbons.

She imagined the woman reading the letter and saying, "Lady Brentwood, never heard of her, I'm afraid. Do you have her telephone number, by any chance?"

She made her exit, slipping out of the door in her borrowed clothes, as Charles gave her a kiss and wished her luck at the door.

CHAPTER FOURTEEN

1956

CHARLES ARRIVES PUNCTUALLY ON HIS BICYCLE. AS HE ENTERS her lounge in the khaki shorts and long socks he still wears, he seems to Bill, endearingly, to look as he did as a boy with his dark hair, worn with a forelock falling into his luminous brown eyes.

Despite all their talk of diets, the four of them repair to the dining room, summoned by the clatter of cutlery, the odors of cooking meat, and the ancient Zulu cook, who announces, "Luncheon is served," grandly, not looking anyone in the eye, doing his duty punctiliously, disdainfully, attired in his starched white uniform with the blue sash that ends in a tassel at his waist. It is clear he considers himself a cut above his present employer and her family, and there are moments like this when she agrees.

He has spread a gleaming white tablecloth across the mahogany table. Blue plumbago spills from a low silver bowl in the center, and the starched napkins rise stiffly like bishops' miters at each plate.

"It all looks lovely," Bill tells him, thinking of his late night and how early he must have risen this morning to prepare this feast.

Charles, who has already betrayed his excited anticipation, rubbing his hands and screwing up his rapacious eyes, gloating, prepares to carve. Indeed, the cook has replaced the chickens he had prepared the day before with a succulent feast. He has laid out a plump roast beef served with Yorkshire pudding on the sideboard, which Charles, after sharpening the carving knife carefully, carves expertly, while the cook passes around the two green vegetables and potatoes and rice.

They all drink several beers under the disapproving eye of the servant. Charles seems almost to purr with pleasure, though all through the meal the conversation continues somewhat lugubriously and suspiciously on the topic of her dead husband. What are they trying to tell her: how grateful she should be to them?

Really, she thinks, the cook is the one who knows most about her—almost as many of her secrets as Gladys does. He understands a great deal more than he says. He has not looked happy since her husband died, and she moved to smaller quarters. She knows his room here is small and windowless and cold in winter. Perhaps she should leave him an annuity. Then she remembers her husband has already done that.

Now he passes around the dessert: a choice of trifle with whipped cream or fruit salad with ice cream. He brings each dish in and lifts off the silver lid solemnly like a magician. Everyone praises his cooking, but he does not respond, going on with the service in disapproving silence.

Pie wipes her mouth with her starched white napkin and leaves a little smear of strawberry on it.

Charles gazes at Bill over his rapidly diminishing trifle. "You've always been so lucky." This is true in some ways: at cards and horses.

She had thought herself particularly lucky that first day at the house on Hume Road, and yet that much luck had troubled her. It was all so surprisingly easy that she felt from the start there was something she did not understand.

CHAPTER FIFTEEN

1935

SHE TOOK THE TRAM AND BUS AND THEN WALKED, SWEATING IN the heat and silence of the afternoon, worrying about stains under the arms of her blouse as well as dust on her shoes, as she went under old shade trees and peered through the thick hedges, catching glimpses of lives which she imagined to be of luxury and ease.

She heard the ping of tennis balls, the muffled splash of water in a pool, someone calling a servant's name. She walked on and entered through the high white gate, which was invitingly thrown open that sun-filled October afternoon. She went up the long driveway under the jacarandas already in bloom, the pale mauve petals falling slowly, it seemed to her, through the still air. All was hushed about her—*the silence of the rich*—she thought, the light brilliant, the air still, the sweet smell of the *yesterday-today-and-tomorrow* bushes, heightened by the sun. She stood between the tubs of purple, mauve, and white flowers which flanked the front door and hesitated to ring the bell, afraid of disturbing the peace of the afternoon.

A tall, dignified servant in a starched white uniform and soft-soled shoes, his narrow head held high like a club, opened the door for her. He stood there and eyed her suspiciously, as well he might have, but allowed her to enter into that hall with the black-and-white tile, the old brass-studded *kist* and the grandfather clock with its gold angels carrying trumpets lifted to the sky. He led her down the steps and waved a white gloved hand toward a cool and dimly lit lounge where the mauve velvet curtains were closed on the afternoon light. He left her, she felt, reluctantly, afraid she might make off with the silver he had polished to such a high shine. With a glance of disapproval, he muttered at the door, "I will tell my madam you are here."

She was not sure whether to sit or stand and hesitated, despite her sore feet, looking around the sweep of the large room with its shining silver, the shimmering Steinway grand piano, left open, music on its stand, the bound books in the bookcases, and open on tables, old portraits on the walls, and pink tiger lilies fanned in glass vases on polished mahogany surfaces, their petals reflected in the wood. She had never seen such a lovely place. How she wanted to possess that room and all that was in it!

Her prospective employer did not keep her waiting long but came down the steps into the lovely lounge, followed by two small black dachshunds with jeweled collars. A slim, tall woman in her late forties, she had shimmering, silvery hair carelessly caught up behind her head in a loose chignon. Like the beautiful room, the slight disorder of her appearance only added to its charm. She wore a simple gray skirt and pale pink-gray shirt, the sleeves rolled up to the elbows, and a gray cardigan slung around her bony shoulders. Though she had obviously made little effort with her dress, she remained elegant and patrician. Everything about her seemed pale: her blue eyes, her skin, her lips, her narrow Italian handmade shoes. Only her dogs were sleek, dark, and bejeweled.

She immediately liked everything about Helen, who introduced herself, her slimness, her perfume, she even liked her little shiny black dogs who sniffed around her legs in a friendly, welcoming way. She had an upper-class accent, but there was nothing haughty or pretentious about her. She even seemed unsure of how to proceed.

She had a tentative, welcoming smile, a tremulous, damp handshake. "Would you like to go into the garden?" she suggested as though she had invited Bill for tea, or as if *she* were the applicant for the position.

They wandered out into the spring garden together and sat under a huge oak tree in yellow deck chairs, sprinklers turning on the green lawn, with a hissing sound. Helen sat rather slumped, as though apologizing for her height, her slim legs and fine ankles in pale silk stockings folded to one side, her slender fingers nervously drumming in her lap, her sleek dogs at her feet.

"There won't be much for you to do. The servants have things pretty much under control," she said, smiling almost apologetically. The servant, who had ostensibly come out to see if they needed anything, was probably checking to see if Bill was behaving decently. Helen asked him to bring a cup of coffee and some biscuits and seemed rather unsure of his response.

Bill sipped the coffee and munched the biscuits greedily, feeling suddenly hungry. She had never tasted such delicious biscuits, ones with sweet cream between flaky pink pastry. Helen talked about the hydrangeas, which were doing so well that year, and about the bulbs she had planted that spring. She spoke of a ten-year-old boy from a previous marriage who had been sent away to boarding school in the Cape.

"My husband thought it would be wise. He feels discipline is very important for a boy," she said rather sadly. She said her husband certainly was a disciplined man, who worked very hard and was often absent, and she waved her hands eloquently around the large garden and toward the big, square house to imply her loss. She sounded lonely, Bill thought, and noticed how Helen surreptitiously slipped a piece of biscuit to each of her dogs. She wondered when the woman would get around to asking her some hard questions or at least for her references, but she just sat there with her fine hands beating a tune in her lap, staring rather dreamily across the lawn, as though there were someone or something out there of interest.

Helen—she reminded Bill to call her that—seemed rather surprised by the whole business of hiring a nurse-companion. When Bill gathered her courage and offered up the reference herself, her heart drumming in her ears, the woman only glanced carelessly at Haze's eloquent sentences, written in her best secretarial style—"To whom it may concern," she had prefaced the letter—and handed it back to Bill. She

mumbled something about Bill coming highly recom-
mended. She made no effort to ask for a telephone number
or even write down the fictive address: "The Paddock,
Morningside Drive, Houghton," they had invented.

It was clear that the idea of this position must have
come from someone else entirely, perhaps from the husband,
though at that point Bill did not understand why. The house
certainly was not disorganized, on the contrary, and nor did
Helen look unwell, though it was true she did not seem
authoritarian in any way. Rather, she seemed kind, intelligent, and sensitive. She had a long white graceful neck, a
large generous mouth, and she held her head slightly to one
side, listening to anything Bill said with more than polite
attention and hesitating thoughtfully before she replied.

She asked her about her family and her life in a way that
made Bill feel she really wanted to know. Bill had never met
anyone like her who had listened and questioned with so
much interest. Conversation was not part of her mother's
repertoire. She used gestures: the clutch of a hand. But
Helen smiled with sympathy when Bill said, quite truthfully, that she had always been very close to her two sisters
and her much younger brother. She added that she had carried him around on her back in a blanket as a child.

Helen rose and looked around the garden in a vague
way. She said, "Well, it's growing quite late. You should
probably go and get your things. I hope you'll be happy
with us."

Bill understood, to her surprise, that she was hired on
the spot and would start that evening. Helen seemed as re-

lieved as she was to have the business over and settled. Before Bill left her to collect her few belongings, Helen held on to her hand for a moment longer than necessary and said, almost pathetically, "I do hope we'll be friends and that you won't miss your family too much."

CHAPTER SIXTEEN

1956

NOW HER FAMILY DRAIN THEIR GLASSES AND SCRAPE THEIR PLATES and stagger to the upstairs bedrooms, except for Charles, who says he'll just have a little lie-down for a moment on the sofa in the lounge, before he goes back to work. Her sisters go into the orderly, well-polished boys' rooms, with the mahogany four-poster beds, the *broderie Anglaise* counterpanes, and all their well-thumbed books from their younger days: *Hardy Boys, Treasure Island, Robinson Crusoe,* and *The Swiss Family Robinson*; the thick encyclopedias they still love to peruse; the books on chess and bridge and mathematics; horse books, sailing books, and the leather-bound classics: Rudyard Kipling and Conrad and Rider Haggard, the Russians and the French authors, and all the other thick tomes by authors unknown to Bill, books she was obliged to read to Phillip when he had the measles when she struggled with all the difficult Russian names. "Darling," she had said, "Can't I read you something else without all these long complicated names I can't pronounce?"

Once, she had gone into Mark's room when he was away at school and opened his desk drawer. She was not sure what she was looking for: a love letter from some girl or a teenage diary that might have explained him to her. Instead, when she opened up the thick black exercise book she found long dry excerpts copied from his books in his neat hand in royal blue ink. A passage from *The Brothers Karamazov* about the terrible suffering of innocent children caught her attention, the inexplicable existence of evil in the world. Is this what he was thinking about? She was chagrined. She had always thought of herself as tenderhearted, moved by any sad story, but only from people she knew, not by some abstract idea of evil and suffering in the world. She saw him then as a fierce revolutionary like the French one he had told her about, who was called "The Incorruptible" and cut off heads right, left, and center, in a desperate attempt to eradicate injustice.

She retreats to her own bedroom and falls immediately into heavy sleep. She dreams of Helen, who floats slowly toward her across the smooth lawn, wearing an incongruous, elegant gray hat with a long feather, a hat someone else wore, an old lady at one of the tables in the boardinghouse where they had moved after Bill's husband's death, who would steal pieces of fruit and slip them into her knitting bag.

Helen's big, pale eyes fill with tears. She whispers into her ear. At first it is unclear what she is saying, though Bill leans toward her, closer and closer. Then she understands: Helen is in pain. "I'll do anything for you," she is saying, slipping a note into Bill's hand.

She wakes with a start, her mouth dry, her heart beating

hard, all the old sadness, the regret and loss, seeping like blood through her veins. She looks at her watch and realizes she has slept for several hours and the heat of the day has abated, but she still feels tired, hot, and unwilling to rise and face the rest of the evening, her family, and Mr. Parks.

CHAPTER SEVENTEEN

✼

1935

HELEN USHERED BILL INTO HER ROOM SAYING, IN A KIND WAY, "I hope you'll be happy here with us."

It looked more like a suite than a room, with its vast view of the garden, romantic in the shadows of the twilight, the big comfortable bed with its many cushions and pillows, under the wide window, and in an alcove, the bookcase with all the blue and maroon leather-bound books, a small blue silk-covered love-seat, and the fold-down mahogany desk. There was even a bouquet of multicolored roses in a round glass vase on a lace doily on the dresser, a cotton dressing gown placed on the bed for her.

That evening, she dined alone with Helen in the long dining room, with its French doors that gave onto the garden. Though a place had been set for the husband at the top of the mahogany table, with the glittering silver and a bowl of white roses from the garden, he had not appeared. Sitting opposite her, Helen seemed nervous, crumbling the center of her roll into small balls but not eating much. She picked fussily at the delicious roast lamb with green peas. She kept glancing at the door and at the corner cupboard in the dining room as though it harbored a thief. She crumpled her linen napkin, rose from the table before the dessert, and drifted toward the door.

Helen had that capacity to hover in life, not just in dreams. Bill thought she looked like an angel as she drifted toward the door, her hair shimmering, looking back over her shoulder, apologizing, putting her long, bejeweled fingers to her forehead delicately.

She claimed she had a migraine, and Bill offered to accompany her to her room, but she waved a fine hand and told her to finish her meal, leaving her alone at the long table. She sat in awkward silence, the cook moving about her with his abrupt, angry gestures, his face showing displeasure at serving her dessert. She was an intruder here. What was her work to be? All sorts of strange possibilities ran through her mind. Whatever the reason, the servant did not approve. Grudgingly, he brought her a small slice of delicious apple pie punctuated with a comma of whipped cream, followed by a demitasse of bitter coffee so hot it burned her tongue. She did not dare ask for sugar or milk.

She was sprawled out in her bra and half petticoat after her long day when she heard the knock on her door. She was considering she might have made a mistake, should probably just pack her suitcase again and go home. The situation seemed too weird.

She was on the wide bed, lying under the fan which turned fast, stirring up the hot night air. She jumped up, fumbled her arm into the sleeve of the gown, and opened the door a crack. The servant who had let her into the house and served dinner was standing there in his white starched uniform, with the blood-red sash across his chest. He informed her solemnly that the master was waiting for her in his study. She dressed quickly and slipped quietly down the stairs. She had already understood the need for discretion. She went through the hall and knocked on what she hoped was the study door.

"Come in," he said in a low, pleasant voice, and she entered a dimly lit, book-lined and paneled study, on the west side of the house, with a dark, heavy leather couch, a gramophone, and green velvet curtains.

He was sitting in the shadows. She could hardly see his face but gathered he was neat from the small stacks of paper on his desk. His cigar lit up his face and perfumed the room. In the green light of the desk lamp and the cigar's glow she did not find his face unattractive, though he was clearly much older than she, nearer her father's age, bright blue-eyed and balding, the forehead, high and white, the hair that remained silvery and neat. He looked uneasy and solemn as he stubbed out his cigar in the large glass ashtray and considered her.

He did not introduce himself but asked her to shut the door. His expression was stern but not indifferent. He was staring at her, consuming her with his gaze, traveling from her face to her feet, in Pie's white shirt and Haze's dark skirt, somewhat rumpled at this point. She had not had time to brush her hair or put on lipstick and, glancing down, she realized she had done up the buttons on the blouse wrong, so that it gaped. She had seen men stare at her like this before, but that was not what he was looking for. He was looking for something particular.

Embarrassed, she forced herself to meet his gaze when he inquired about her age. She considered telling him it was none of his business or diminishing it, as she sometimes did, but thought that age might be an advantage here. She confessed she was twenty-seven.

She was accustomed to people who did not know her giving her some compliment about her looks and expressing wonderment at her availability, something she would ignore, if she could. "A beauty like you and not married yet? You must be a difficult woman," they said with a teasing smile. But he did not smile and only said, after a pause, "Good— not too young or impressionable, I gather. And not too easily persuaded," a remark which seemed incomprehensible and rude. He went on, unperturbed by her silence, "My wife tells me you have a good reference?"

She would have liked to tell him it was up to him to find out, but she simply nodded and continued to stare back into his avid, intelligent eyes. "Anyway, she likes you, and that's the main thing, here," he said, grinning in a surprisingly frank, youthful, and mischievous way.

She could see he had a sense of humor, of fun. Also, there was a glimmer of complicity in his blue eyes. She felt he knew all about her, had immediately guessed her secrets— the subterfuge, the false reference—or something about her past that would be useful to him—the youthful indiscretion, the love affair, perhaps a scandal.

Still, she felt at ease. There was no need to pretend. She

moved a little closer to his desk, twisted her wide gold slave-bracelet around her arm and smiled at him.

"Are you able to get up early in the morning and keep my wife company until eight or nine in the evening when I get back from work? I don't want her to be alone for a moment."

"I am an early riser. I'd be happy to keep her company," she said. She did not think Helen would be bad company, and she was used to the continuous presence of others—enjoyed it, even. She thought this man must have realized, as she had, that his wife was lonely in their huge house and garden. She was touched by his solicitude. What a thoughtful, loving husband. She presumed the advantage of being rich was that you could pay for companionship.

"Good," he said. Then he stretched out a hand with something in it and whispered, "I'm going to give these to you. I'm away so much of the time, because of my work, and naturally I cannot rely on the servants to have the authority . . ." For a moment he hesitated, closed his fist and put it to the cleft in his chin. She moved a little closer to him in the shadowy room to see what he had there, as he said, "I suppose you're not the sort of person who loses things."

"No," she said, because until then she had not had many things to lose, though she had once lost the most essential.

The family had no car. She had no jewelry to speak of, though she had always kept, wrapped up carefully in tissue paper in a drawer, an amber necklace from Isaac. But in their house, none of the doors locked, even the outhouse had no lock.

He opened up his hand, and named each of the keys on the ring: for the pantry cupboards, for the store cupboards; for the servants' bin of mealie meal; for the flour bin; for the liquor cabinet in the dining room.

"All of them? Is this necessary?" she asked, coming closer, hesitating, trying to understand.

He pressed the key ring firmly into the palm of her hand and folded her small fingers over it with his warm, strong ones, clamping her fingers shut. She recalled the clerk giving Isaac the big key to the room in the old hotel and felt a little shudder run through her body, as he said, "You must keep the doors locked; it is important, you understand?"

His own wife, she thought, beginning to comprehend. He doesn't trust his own wife.

He let her hand go, and she took the keys from him and stood looking down on them, each one with its identifying tag, neatly marked in blue ink.

CHAPTER EIGHTEEN

1956

From her bed she hears a scratching on her door. "Who is it?" she asks.

The cook, coming in with the tea tray, says her brother wants to talk to her.

"Shall I tell him to go away?" he asks.

"Oh, just tell him to come in," she says, and sighs crossly, propping herself up on her pillows. She mutters to herself as much as to the cook as she takes her teacup from him, "All I'm fit for apparently is to help this family of mine." He shakes his head and clucks his tongue with sympathy and disapproval at her family's demands.

Uninvited, Charles pushes his dark head through the open doorway and asks to come in. He hangs his head and rustles the papers he holds behind his back. He stands close beside her, looking embarrassed as usual, and grinning his guilty grin. He sits down beside her on the edge of her bed, refusing her offer of tea. He strokes her hand as he speaks.

"Sometimes, I regret what happened—you know what

I mean? I have always tried to help you, to think what would be best for you, for all of us," he says.

She has often confided in him from an early age, telling him what was going through her mind. It saved a lot of time to talk to him. She did not have to explain things. She felt he understood their mother's inability to cope with anything, her helpless collusion with their father, his rigidity, his self-righteousness. She had even confided in him when he was such a young boy and she was just seventeen and so much in love and had lost what was dearest to her.

She has always felt he gave her remarkably sensible advice, though she was sometimes reluctant to follow it. Though he doesn't seem to have used it much in his own life, he is not devoid of common sense.

"I tried to give you good advice when you came to me on your Sundays off, and we talked," he says.

"Rather, I talked," she says, grinning at him and looking into his dark eyes and wondering why he is reminding her.

CHAPTER NINETEEN

1935

She talked endlessly to Charles when she left the house
on Hume Road and went home on her first Sunday off,
a month after her arrival there. After the big family Sunday luncheon, the air was still redolent with the smells of the
homecoming meal: boiled beef, cabbage, carrots, and bread
pudding with custard, the heavy English food that her
mother liked, which was so unsuitable to the hot climate.
She lounged luxuriously on the old leather sofa beside him,
her hands empty, her bare feet up on a low stool, the thin
curtains no protection from the bright light.

They talked, while their mother and sisters clattered
away in the kitchen, washing the dishes, and their father
took his nap in the summer heat. Now that she had brought
back her first month's salary, she was not called upon to wash
dishes or help with the sewing that was still being done by
the others. She was happy to be able to talk with her atten-
tive brother. Together they smoked Craven "A" cigarettes,
opening the windows and fanning away the smoke, so that

their father would not smell it when he eventually staggered forth after his nap.

"So how's the job going?" Charles asked Bill and took a piece of tobacco from his tongue. She told him how the husband was always following her or having her come to him. She would smell his Cuban cigar whenever he was in the house, a scent that trailed after him like a train. He would waylay her to question her in the morning, coming upon her suddenly in the narrow passageway with the series of etchings of London scenes, Wheatley's *Cries of London* on the walls.

He appeared to be everywhere, emerging unexpectedly, coming around corners. "I'm always bumping into him," she told Charles. He strode, long-legged, around the many rooms of the big house in his pale Sulka shirts and elegant English shoes. He switched off lights and turned off taps that had been left on. He expected her to earn her generous pay. He whispered to her often in his low, persuasive voice, Listerine lingering on his breath.

"He asks me about her, and sometimes I don't know what to tell him," she said.

"Say as little as possible if you want to keep your job," Charles counseled. "Just tell him what he wants to hear: that everything's fine."

"But it's not fine at all," she protested. She wanted to keep both her large salary and the beautiful blue room where she slept alone in the large bed and her own clean bathroom, where she bathed at night, luxuriously lingering in the scented water, singing. She had fallen rather in love with Helen, and she was not sure what was wrong with her, why she was so dependent, why her husband worried so about her. She understood that he and she were allies in a precarious game, though she did not yet realize just how precarious.

She related how she had gone to Helen's big bedroom that first morning early, as she had been instructed to do, just as soon as she heard the husband's Rolls Royce go down the driveway. She found the door closed and stood listening for a moment to the silence within. Then she knocked softly and said, "It's me," and then hesitated when she heard no response. She remembered the husband's instructions and knocked again more forcefully and then opened the door softly, entering the darkened room.

She found Helen sitting at her dressing table in a cream lace bra, silk half-petticoat, and fluffy cream slippers, her fine, silver hair loose on her shoulders, her head drooping like a snowdrop, a picture of delicate dejection. The little black dogs watched her warily from their kidney-shaped bed. The breakfast tray of fruit and oatmeal and coffee in its shiny silver pitcher stood untouched on the bed. She was weeping silently but when she caught sight of Bill, she rose and walked restlessly around the room.

Bill tried to think of what to say or do to cheer her. She asked what plans she had for the day. When Helen did not reply, on an impulse she picked up the fat Russian book that lay by her bedside and offered to read aloud, turning the pages, with all the long unpronounceable names.

"What's the point of it all?" Helen asked at last. She said her whole body ached as if she had the flu. "If you knew what it was like to wake each morning and find yourself there with the same old dull ache," she said despairingly. She went on talking of the absurdity of her life, the pointlessness of her existence, with all these servants, who did everything for her. She said nothing appealed to her. What purpose would it serve? It all seemed so senseless.

Bill found this list of mysterious complaints rather fascinating and exotic, perhaps because she had always had good health and had had to work for a living. In Helen's presence, she suddenly felt veils lift, her family's oppressive laws repealed. Yes, she thought, this is where I want to be.

She suggested they might spend their afternoons in the cinema, as she had done as a girl, taking the tram into Johannesburg to see Rudolph Valentino in *The Sheik*, but Helen demurred.

She wanted to make Helen happy. She understood that her job depended on it. Besides, she did not want her to be unhappy. She wanted people to be happy around her. She felt obligated to make them so. If they were not, she must try harder; it was one of her failings.

She wanted Helen to like her, and she was willing to apply herself to make that happen. "So what did you finally do?" Charles asked.

She replied that she chattered on about whatever came to mind: clothes, food, music, and even books, though, of course, she had read very few, and Helen had read many— she had an English degree from Cape Town University. She could read French and Italian and spoke to the servants in fluent Zulu.

Though school had seemed a waste of time to Bill, she had read during her time in her aunts' house. *The Mill on the Floss* was one of her favorites, she told Helen. She said she had read certain books she had only seen on the shelf in the husband's study.

Helen asked Bill if she had read *Jude the Obscure*. "So sad—those poor children," Helen said, and Bill pulled a sad face though she had never opened the book.

She made up stories, exaggerated, embroidered a little on the truth, and Helen listened attentively as they walked arm in arm, through the light and shade of the lovely garden. Helen watched her with her large pale blue eyes, clearly amused and moved by her efforts. She would put her arm around Bill's waist, her aching head on her shoulder, saying, "I want to be good for my husband, to do the right thing."

Bill told Helen how fat she had been as a child, how greedy, how she had taken the money she had been given to buy school shoes and instead, bought a whole box of cream cakes which she ate on her way home in the tram. In those days the children would call out to her, "Oh, fat white lady whom no one loves, why do you walk through the fields in white gloves." She made Helen laugh.

She came to confide in Helen, sharing her secret about her love affair with a Jewish man when she was seventeen. "My parents didn't approve, and they had the marriage annulled," she said.

One particularly beautiful morning, she asked hopefully if they could play something on the gramophone. She loved to listen to the latest musicals. Helen smiled at her, asking how she managed to be so endlessly cheerful.

She coaxed her into her clothes and got her downstairs into the study where she opened the curtains on the day. She put on a record, rolled up the carpet, and took her by the hand. "Dance with me," she said, leading her across the parquet floor, twisting and turning her supple body in her mauve cotton shirtwaist dress, her full skirt blooming around her, rising and dipping, while Ethel Merman sang "I've got rhythm" on the gramophone. How she loved to dance! She was sure Helen was enjoying herself, too, with the windows thrown open on the vast smooth lawn, the sounds of the mower, and the smell of freshly cut grass, the two of them laughing like children.

In the evenings she persuaded Helen to play the Steinway for her and was able to enjoy classical music for the first time: Brahms, Mozart, and even Bach.

She convinced her once to take a drive into town in the green Chevrolet, the two of them sitting talking in the shadows in the back seat. She even persuaded her to swim, one hot day in November, in the large cool pool. She coaxed her, though frightened, into the cool water.

The husband had come back one evening while they were swimming. She looked up and saw him striding across the smooth lawn with his cigar glowing in his hand in the twilit garden. They swam back and forth, as she watched him. He told them about his work that day at the timberyard in Johannesburg, which he had started as a young man on his own. He smiled down at her with satisfaction from the edge of the pool when she stopped swimming. He reached down a hand to help her out.

She stood there, pulling off her cap, shaking out her hair, the water streaming off her soft, curvaceous body. He came a little closer and whispered in her ear, "Good work," and squeezed her hand.

CHAPTER TWENTY

1935

SHE WAS ONLY ABLE TO DISTRACT HELEN FROM HER SORROWS briefly, and as the days went by, a hot, still December settled down upon them.

"If I could just keep moving, moving all the time," Helen would suddenly say, sitting beside her in the back of the Chevrolet. When the chauffeur drove them into town, she would put her hands to her head and exclaim, "Such an awful buzzing in my head. If you only knew!"

One morning, Bill strode into her bedroom without knocking, her keys jangling importantly at her waist. This time Helen gave her an impatient glance, adding, "You might knock, you know. Am I not allowed any privacy?" She sat before her dressing table with her arms crossed and complained that she was no longer mistress in her own house; she was bereft of any importance; the servants were laughing at her.

Bill went over to her and sat down on the long stool beside her, taking her hand. "Why would they laugh at you?"

Helen lifted her drooping head and looked her in the eye, saying, "I don't think you understand what's going on here. What has my husband told you?" Bill looked down guiltily as Helen fingered the keys at her waist. What right had she to them? Why did she have to be in constant attendance?

Helen looked at her more narrowly and seemed to be considering. She said, "He's impossible, you know. I knew it from the first moment I met him."

"How did you meet him?" Bill asked.

She related how old friends, worried about her, had introduced them. She told her what sounded at first like the whole story, though afterward it was clear she had left out the most important parts.

She had been desperately in love with her first husband, a lanky blond Englishman, a talented artist. One morning he had told her he couldn't think of the word for the thing you push a baby in. "You mean a pram?" she had said, staring at him. He was dead of a brain tumor within three months. He left her with nothing but her little boy and a mountain of debt. He had not even paid the rent for the charming thatch-roofed cottage where they had lived in someone else's garden, nor the poor servant who had helped her with her little boy.

As a child she had been a musical prodigy but was never good enough to become a professional. She had started writing and even published a story in a women's magazine. But she needed security. She could not work, even as a secretary. She was not a good typist. Teaching did not pay enough.

Her friends had invited her to dinner and placed her on the right of this tall, balding, good looking, elegantly dressed, somewhat older man. From the start he had admonished her to eat up and not to drink so much wine. He insisted on driving her home, and when he got her there, of course, he wanted to come in "for a nightcap." Then she managed to get rid of him—or she thought she had, for when she woke the next morning, she found he had returned—she never locked the doors—and filled the place with huge baskets of red roses. Everywhere she looked there were these enormous baskets of red roses. In one of them he had left a note saying. "I'll be back at five," as though she had no choice.

He both thrilled and terrified her. He insisted on taking her out the next evening to an expensive restaurant; he wanted to present her with jewels, a beautiful pearl necklace, the pearls as big as cherries. She protested, but he had understood what she needed.

He had shown her his house: the grand piano open, the books, the flowers, the silent smiling servants in their white suits—who would not fall for all that?

She had accepted, and he had taken care of everything, including her boy, his nanny, and then his private schooling.

Then he pressed further demands on her. He insisted on her being present whenever he needed her. She was never free to lead her own life. She had to attend all his business dinners, his endless trips, to go to bed and to rise when he did. He wouldn't consider her working. "What on earth would you want to work for?" he said.

"But I want to write," she said.

"I don't want you writing some book where I will undoubtedly find myself in some unflattering form," he said.

He insisted on sex at odd moments and in odd places. He

would sometimes come back from work unexpectedly, and surprise her when she was working in the garden. She would be there in the sun in her straw hat and gardening gloves and old thick shoes. He would take her wordlessly by the hand and lead her across the lawn, push her into the gardening shed, and force her down on her hands and knees in the dirt. He would rip at her clothes, and thrust himself into her from behind like a wild beast. Or he would come at her when she was playing the piano in the evening and drag her up the stairs to the bedroom and push her against the wall. "Standing up like stallions," he would say. He would prod and push at her with his long fingers. She would have to utter the awful things he wanted.

Afterward, she would get into the bath and scrub at her skin until it was pink, to get rid of his smell, his lingering presence, her shame.

He was insanely jealous, always imagining she was off with other men. She could not even drive into town on her own. She was not allowed to go down to the Cape to visit her boy in boarding school. She missed her old artistic friends, interesting people, intellectuals, people who talked about ideas, politics, the color bar. Without them, without anyone to share her work with, she was unable to write.

She considered Bill her jailor, a spy, a snitch, who reported on her. She took her hand from Bill's and looked at her. Bill tried to think of what to say in response. "I'm not your jailor!" she exclaimed, looking into Helen's pale eyes, but she was precisely that. She had all the keys. They never left her presence. Everywhere she went they jingled along with her. And she was always with Helen every moment of the day as she had promised she would be.

"I'll leave if you want me to," she said. "I don't want this role."

Helen sighed and said, "You don't understand: that wouldn't change anything. He'd only find someone else, and at least I like you. You're like a breath of fresh air here."

CHAPTER TWENTY-ONE

✢

1956

CHARLES WIPES HIS MOUTH AND PULLS ON HIS DARK FORELOCK, apologetically. "Sorry to worry you again, but I don't know who else to turn to," he says.

"What can I do for you?" she says as she always ends up doing, looking up at him, her old friend who would come when she screamed in the night, seeing an angel at the bottom of her bed, the one who called her father to get her loose when she stuck her head between the brass bars at the end of the bed.

"I wonder if you could help me with this?" he asks, shifting nearer to her, sidling up on the bed, and thrusting the papers into her lap as her children once did with her diamonds. "I'm afraid I'm rather short again this month. Don't know how it happened."

"That pitiful salary they pay you is just never enough," she says. She glances down at his many bills, stapled to a list of figures with the grand total at the end. His wife has bought a new suite of furniture for her lounge. Bill frowns and worries that she is not helping her brother by always paying his bills. But what else can she do?

She tells him to get her checkbook out of the drawer in the dressing table and writes him a check to cover the amount of his bills.

"You're a little mother to me, Bill," Charles murmurs, as he always does, and kisses her on both cheeks.

"I am going to make sure you are always taken care of," she says. "I'm going to tell Parks," she adds.

"You better give him ten thousand pounds to satisfy him, to keep him quiet, if you want him to carry out your wishes," he adds before he leaves, getting up fast, and whistling as he bicycles down the road, heading back to his wife, who has a large appetite for fancy furniture.

CHAPTER TWENTY-TWO

✻

1936

ONE AFTERNOON, SHE LOST HELEN. IT WAS A WARM SUMMER'S day in January, when she had been employed for three months. They were sitting in the garden in the yellow deck chairs, sipping coffee from gilt-rimmed demitasses after a heavy luncheon. It was a peaceful moment: a bee buzzed, a servant sang as he worked, and she was smiling at Helen. She caught a glimpse of how she must have looked when she was very young, her eyes full of curiosity, her hair light, her pale skin smooth. She wondered how that lively girl had become such a lonely woman, one who seemed to have lost hope. Then she closed her eyes on the glitter of sunlight and must have dozed.

She awoke with a start and looked around, seeing only the leghorn hat, the coffee cup with the lipstick on the rim, and the book Helen had been reading lying in the grass. She panicked and rushed up the bank to the pool.

It occurred to her at that moment and quite clearly that what Helen suffered from was depression, and that her husband was not the tyrant she had portrayed but concerned, afraid his wife might try to take her own life some day. Her complaints all made sense in this light as well: her feelings of uselessness, her lack of purpose, her listlessness.

She ran on breathlessly through the beds of white roses, glittering in the bright light; all the sounds of the sunlit place, the buzzing of the bees over the flowers, the chirring of the cicadas, the cry of a bird, as well as the drumming of her heart, coming to her. She stood at the edge of the pool, staring down into the flickering light, as the oak tree's branches swayed above. For a brief moment she thought she saw a shadow on the bottom.

Then she ran across the lawn to the house, thinking of other possibilities: kitchen knives, gas, or even, who knew? a hidden gun. She recalled a book Helen had been reading, where a man whose mind was damaged during the war commits suicide by throwing himself out a window in London. She looked up at the windows, but they were closed and shuttered in the heat. She went in through the kitchen door into the large kitchen where the servants were busy preparing dinner, rolling butter between serrated wooden slats, kneading dough, or basting the roast beef. They did not stop their work, but simply stared at her in silence when she asked them if they had seen their mistress. She went on through the long passageway, through the still lounge and dining room, the very portraits, the shining silver, the flowers fanned in cut-glass vases seeming to mock her. She galloped up the green-carpeted stairs two at a time and along the corridor, hearing the sound of running water.

She followed it until she stood before the master bathroom door. She imagined Helen inside in the bath, her wrists slit, expiring. She could hear water running inside. She tried the door, but it was locked. "Helen!" she called, rattling the doorknob desperately. Eventually she took out her ring of keys and, fumbling, her hands trembling, went through them until she found the right one.

At first, in the big steamy white-and-black tiled room, she could see only the outline of the big bathtub and behind the shower curtain a vague silhouette. "Helen?" she said tentatively, tiptoeing over to the bath. "Are you alright?" But there was no response. Then she pulled back the curtain with one quick movement.

Helen was sitting naked in the hot water, her hair pinned up on top of her head, beads of sweat on her face, her head tilted back, the steam rising around her. But there was no blood. She was not exsanguinating. She was sitting in the hot bath grinning, guzzling a large bottle of gin. Bill reached across and took the bottle from her and poured the little that was left down the basin. Helen looked at her, bleary-eyed, giggling. She took her arm and lifted her out of the bath, wrapped a thick towel around her dripping body, helped her into the bedroom, and dried off her slender white curves. She could not help noticing the youthful form, the firm breasts, untouched by maternity. She put her into her bed, pulled the sheet over her. She lay there giggling for a moment and then seemed to fall asleep.

PART THREE

CHAPTER TWENTY-THREE

1956

IT IS EARLY ON A WARM AFTERNOON, A WEEK SINCE MR. PARKS'S visit. She has still not decided what to do about her will, but she knows she cannot continue this way.

Today, both her boys are home for their Sunday off, but they will have to return to school shortly. They have all eaten a large luncheon, the boys stuffing themselves with roast chicken and roast potatoes, along with fruit salad and ice cream, to please the cook. He has stood over them, chuckling contentedly and going back and forth from the sideboard to the table, clicking the bottle opener against the bottles to see which ones they prefer: Coca-Cola or sparkling lemon.

"So," she says and looks at her boys across the table. Fruit flies hover over the heaped fruit bowl in the center of the table as they would do at the house on R Street. She sips beer to give herself courage. Her heart hammers as she begins, "There is something I need to tell you."

How little she has told her boys! They seem so good to

her, so hardworking, such Boy Scouts. She so wants them to love and admire her.

They sit up straight, in their white cotton shirts and gray shorts—neither of them will wear the bright-colored shirts she buys them—pale hair falling in their faces, pink with the sun and indignation, their long fingers folded on the table, waiting expectantly to hear what she has to say to them.

She is not sure how to proceed. Perhaps if they were girls, it would be easier. Girls are easier to talk to, more forgiving, surely. Her boys' lives have been so different from her own: children of privilege. She is afraid that if she delays, someone else will tell them, Mr. Parks, perhaps, his pink upper lip peeking through his mustache.

She has told the cook to take a few hours off.

"What is it?" Phillip asks, his eyes bright with curiosity.

She gathers herself up and says, "You really only fall in love once in your life." They look at her blankly: what do they know about falling in love? She sips from her glass and tries again. She announces that she had been married before she married their father.

"Why didn't you tell us?" Phillip asks.

She explains that she had run away from home at seventeen—the same age Mark is now—because her parents, she knew, would not have approved of her choice, would never have allowed her to marry him, or anyone else for that matter. So, she had eloped.

"You mean you actually climbed out of a window and ran away?" Phillip asks. Bill nods her head.

"How romantic!" Mark says and clasps his long, fine fingers, batting his white eyelashes.

"It sounds like a story out of a book," Phillip says enthusiastically. He wants to know more: "Who was he?"

She had expected a disapproving silence, not eager questions and delight. She should have realized her boys might be interested. She is not sure how to answer their questions. She has misjudged them. She is unsettled by their curiosity, and not prepared to divulge more.

She says his name was Isaac and he was Jewish.

"Really! A Jewish man!" Phillip says, obviously delighted at the thought. For him, Jews are all intellectuals. He admires them.

She nods. She tells them that Isaac was not much older than they are now, a tall, freckled redhead. "He had a wonderful beard," she says and puts her hand to her cheek and smiles at the memory. She can see all of this delights them, but not for the reasons which delighted her.

"He could sing 'Tea for Two' and 'I Want to Be Happy,' though not actually very well." She laughs.

She met him in her father's office and fell hopelessly in love with him. He was a man who, like their grandfather, knew all about gems, who spent his days staring through a loupe.

"What happened?" Phillip wants to know.

Carried away by their enthusiasm, she says that the loupe fell from his eye as he looked up at her. She does not remember that exactly, but perhaps it did.

She leaves out the most important parts of the story, feeling her cheeks flush, and talks about the aunts instead.

"The ones who couldn't marry because of their father's will?" Mark says.

"That's right."

Kimberley in those days was filled with people who came there to make their fortunes on diamonds or any other way possible, she tells them. She never really believed the aunts' story but cousins confirmed it, telling her they were always sending over suitors to try and tempt the girls to marry and relinquish the money, though ironically there was never much money.

Phillip laughs and says he remembers going to their house with the long, dark shotgun corridor and the garden out the back with the fig tree. He went out into the garden and picked the figs that had dropped to the ground. The three aunts had cooed and fussed over him and Mark, touching their hair, their cheeks, and their hands as though they were something precious.

"Diamonds, they thought you were diamonds," she says.

CHAPTER TWENTY-FOUR

‥

1925

"It's for the best," Aunt Winnie said, bringing a tray of bread and cheese, a few figs, and a glass of sherry for her as she lay there alone, weeping in her dark room. "You'll meet a lovely man of our faith, who will marry you in the church where you were baptized and confirmed, and where you belong, and you'll start your life again."

But she continued to weep, without lifting her head, and when her aunt had left the room, she placed the tray on the floor. She might as well starve. She was convinced she could never start her life again. How could she, ever?

She was right about that, though she did not, at first, realize how much had changed.

Coming into the dining room one morning, after four miserable weeks in that house, smelling the porridge that was served for breakfast, with a thin sprinkling of brown sugar, she was perspiring and nauseated. The aunts stared at her and at one another suspiciously, raising their eyebrows. Aunt May asked if she didn't feel well. "I feel sick," she said, "I must have eaten something that disagreed with me," though she had never had a delicate stomach and indeed, had eaten little since she came into the house.

Despite the appearances of propriety—the neat white picket fence, the flower beds, the family silver, the aproned servant—there was, she had come to understand, over the first few weeks in her aunts' house, increasingly little money to go around, to keep up the old house with its wide floorboards and sash windows and the small garden and to feed and clothe the three women and Gladys who was, she understood, an essential part of the household.

Clearly it was unthinkable for the aunts to consider undertaking any of the chores of cleaning a house or even making their beds themselves. They spent their days embroidering, knitting, or reading the Bible. Even the marketing was done by Gladys, who went off early with her basket on her arm, her strict instructions, and the neat list written with Aunt Maud's old fountain pen with its royal blue ink, the small quantities spelled out exactly and the small sum of money carefully folded in her pocket. The aunts would occasionally go out into the garden in the cool evenings in their large, battered straw hats with veils to protect their delicate white skin and gardening gloves for their small hands, to tend to their flowers and more importantly their vegetable garden, but even there, Gladys was asked to do the weeding, down on her knees, as she was obliged to do all the cooking, albeit under the aunts' strict supervision.

"I can't eat this," she exclaimed now as Gladys passed her a plate of the gray porridge. There was an ominous silence as all three aunts looked at her. She looked back at them, shut her eyes, and for a moment saw a red sun in the blackness. She rose, excused herself, and left the table precipitously, rushing to the cloakroom at the end of the corridor, where she and Isaac had washed their dusty hands on that first evening in the house. Now she vomited bile.

What did this mean, she wondered uneasily, leaning on the basin and looking at her pale, sweating face in the mirror in the small green room. She wished, as she had been doing since her arrival here, that she could escape this house. In her mind, still filled with fairy stories from her childhood, part of her had expected Isaac to rescue her from this prison like the prince who comes through the forest to awaken Sleeping Beauty.

But there was always at least one of her three aunts watching over her, with a severe eye. She had no money, no way of taking a train. Even if she could, she knew she would not be welcome at home, and she knew no one who would help her in the town. She spent her days with her aunts in a miasma of disapproving silence. She longed to be at least alone. Here, it was rarely the case, except for an hour or two in the long, hot afternoons, when all five women would retire to their small rooms under the corrugated roof to rest, when Bill could take off her clothes, sprawl on her bed, and read some dull book from the restricted store her aunts had on their shelves.

Unable to eat much, she realized she was losing weight. What was wrong with her? She would die at seventeen of a broken heart like a heroine in a book.

Aunt Winnie knocked on her door one afternoon when she was resting on her bed with a book. Winnie closed the door behind her, looking pink in the face, embarrassed.

"Is something the matter?" Bill asked.

"No, no dear, well, I hope not," and the silence resumed. Then Winnie said, "We just wanted to make sure, you see. We just wanted to make sure," and looked at Bill as though she could finish her sentence.

"Sure about what?" Bill asked, but she knew then what was coming was not something she wanted to know. In the back of her mind she thought, this cannot be happening to me. She saw her aunt in her pale dress, shiny on the shoulders from repeated wear, with the red lights in her wavy white hair loose down her back, almost like a prim, middle-aged angel in a painting, but no angel of mercy, no angel bringing blessed news.

Aunt Winnie cleared her throat and asked in a low whisper if she had found the rags kept in the bottom drawer, and her gaze indicated the dresser against the wall.

"Yes, I found them there," Bill said, feeling herself flush and obliged to thank her aunt for thinking of her monthly needs.

"We were concerned. You see, it is more than six weeks you have been with us, child, and we haven't seen them hung out to dry on the washing line," Aunt Winnie said, and added, licking at her dry lips before she spoke, "Perhaps you used them and hung them inside out of modesty?" Bill looked at her aunt and said in a faltering voice that she had not needed any rags as of yet, but it was obvious to her as she spoke, even in her ignorance, and her desire not to confront the situation, and certainly it was obvious to her aunt, she could see by her widened eyes and pinched lips, just what her situation was.

Afterward, she noticed how the aunts whispered amongst themselves and stared at her sideways. A suspicious silence spread around her like a stain.

One afternoon, she stood outside the lounge and heard her aunts talking on the telephone discussing her fate with her father. "Under the circumstances she had best remain out of the way, here with us," she heard Aunt Maud say in a doleful tone. "We'll manage somehow, Robert," Aunt Winnie said, in a low pained voice, having taken the phone.

When their conversation was concluded, all three sisters hovering around the telephone, rather like moths around a flame, and Aunt May had sent her brother her love, Bill came into the room and demanded that her aunts tell her what was happening.

They just looked at her in silence and a sort of stunned disbelief. She asked if she might use the phone to speak to her family herself. Aunt Maud stared at her and brushed away a wisp of white hair from her mouth. She said, "We would prefer that you don't use our telephone. In fact it might be better if you do not communicate with anyone."

"It would be more prudent if no one knew your whereabouts," Aunt May said, standing in the dimly lit lounge, the shutters drawn down, her face in the shadows.

"No one?" Bill asked.

"We would prefer that you don't send letters to anyone, not even your sisters or your little brother, especially not to him. We think it would be best for everyone if your presence is not announced in our house. Under the circumstances, we ask you to be as discreet as possible, for our sake as well as your own," Aunt Winnie concluded.

She just stared at her three aunts, standing in a row, like a wall. She turned on her heel, determined to do everything she could to disobey. How could they keep her a prisoner, incommunicado, here for months and months? She could surely convince Gladys to help her, or she would get to a postbox in the night. She would write to her sisters and beg them to send her money. She would write to Isaac.

Sitting crossed-legged on the bed in her tiny back room, she determined to tell Isaac of her predicament. At the same time she thought of the look of disgust and hate in his dark eyes as he had left the room, leaving her in her father's clinging arms. She was not sure that the existence of a child would change his feelings toward her. Clearly, he must have felt she had betrayed his trust, let him down at perhaps the most important moment in his life. She was afraid that he, too, like her aunts and despite his implication in it, would only regard her predicament with disgust.

Continuously she eyed the telephone, but as the days went by and she heard nothing from him, he seemed increasingly like a dream. Had he forgotten her? Sometimes, she dreamed of him, felt his hands on her in the bed beside her, and thought she heard a tap on the windowpane. She even looked out the window to see if he were there. Again and again, she relived the night they had spent together in the hotel. Sometimes, lying alone on her bed in the afternoon, she wondered if she had dreamed the whole affair. She knew so little about him.

CHAPTER TWENTY-FIVE

1925–26

She managed to write to her family, but she received no response. She was never sure if her father was intercepting her letters.

Nor was she to receive any messages or Christmas wishes. She knitted what she could for her aunts, with the wool they provided: striped scarves, tea cozies, and socks, sweating in the heat. Gladys produced a roast chicken on Christmas day which she had stuffed and decorated with a sprig of holly. Bill was allowed to accompany her aunts to church that day and drink a glass of sherry before she went to bed. "Happy Christmas," they said to her, and she felt their gaze on her as she made her way in silence to the back bedroom and the narrow iron bed where she slept. Increasingly she took refuge in long hours of sleep, dreaming and waking, her pillow damp with sweat.

One hot afternoon, in February, when she came in from a walk into town with Aunt Winnie—she was never permitted to go out alone—Aunt Maud greeted her with, "It would be better not to go out there in daylight anymore. We don't want any unnecessary gossip."

Also, at some point, Aunt Maud gave her a bolt of ugly dark blue fabric. "Here, take this. You had better make yourself something that will fit," she said, looking at Bill's swelling stomach.

The aunts, whom she had hoped would be complicit in her love affair, could not have been less understanding. They seemed to regard her as a sort of eyesore, turning their affronted gazes from her when she entered a room in silence. Like small children who close their eyes on what they would like to go away, the aunts seemed to feel that if they did not speak of Bill's condition, or make any reference to future plans, they could make it go away or at least keep it carefully hidden.

She gathered she was a source of embarrassment, a perpetual reminder of what they had forgone. She only added a burden to their already strained circumstances, not only the risk of scandal and shame but also, quite simply, another mouth to feed. The aunts came to regard her, she understood, as a daily affront to all they considered sacred: honor, dignity, and pride, to their upright and cloistered way of life. She was nothing but trouble, trouble brought on them by her thoughtlessness, her lack of control, a weakness of will, her moral deficiency.

After dinner she and Gladys often shuffled along in the dark in sullen silence like two prisoners chained together, when Gladys would no doubt have preferred to put up her feet in her room and rest. Her aunts set the tone in this as in all things.

Food was severely limited, and as she grew larger and the nausea passed, she was increasingly hungry. She craved something more substantial than the breakfast of lumpy Scotch porridge with a thin sprinkle of brown sugar, washed down with a weak cup of tea, or the watery vegetables from the garden she was served for lunch, occasionally accompanied by a thin slice of haddock or kipper, or sometimes a sliver of boiled chicken breast, followed by a few figs from the garden. The vegetables turned up again in the evening in the form of a watery soup, sometimes with a rusk, or followed by a flavorless Marie biscuit.

Sometimes, in desperation, she would slip into the kitchen on the pretext of helping Gladys with the preparations. She would wash and chop the vegetables, the kind she had always hated: anemic turnips, parsnips, or celery root, or as a special treat, a potato. She would help to wash the dishes, hoping to find a few scraps left on the plates to eat. Gladys would try to smuggle her a piece of cheddar cheese, bought with her own savings, which Bill would accept anyway and consume gluttonously in her room.

She craved meat, poultry, fat, cream, and butter. Even bread was rarely put on the table. Her aunts, whether through economy or preference, bought a sort of flat, unleavened, and flavorless English cracker which was served, butterless, with the meals.

She dreamed of thick slices of bread and butter with strawberry jam, of flaming Christmas pudding with currants and a glass of beer. She remembered the dinner she and Isaac had consumed that night so gleefully: the fat sausages, the thick slices of cheese.

On her eighteenth birthday in May, when she was seven months pregnant, she was allowed to receive a little stack of letters of good wishes from her family and even to speak to them on the telephone. Her father wished her a happy day and said that he had sent a check to the aunts to arrange some small festivities. She was allowed two scrambled eggs with bacon and several pieces of toast with butter for her breakfast. For afternoon tea a small cake, iced with granadilla—her favorite—was brought forth. Never had anything tasted so good to her. She cut a piece and took it to Gladys in the kitchen.

The aunts sat around the tea table and ate their slices in silence as she sat there, tears of anger in her eyes, hugely pregnant in the dark blue smock.

Increasingly, she felt she was no one, without a friend or family, an empty shell. Despite her swelling body, or because of it, she had become disembodied. She watched herself from afar, hearing a voice in her head recording her actions, as though she were writing a chronicle of someone else's empty existence. *Now she puts on a straw hat; she steps out into the garden to help Gladys with the weeding.* She had become an observer, a swollen hungry ghost watching herself. Despite her familiarity with these small shuttered rooms she now felt that nothing was a part of her; she was in a timeless and placeless limbo where there was nothing to look forward to.

Without Gladys, she is convinced, she would not have survived. She would talk to her while she worked at her side in the kitchen. They spoke of mundane things: the weather, her health, or something in the paper which her aunts borrowed from the neighbors. She told her about the new pulsating machines that were being used to separate the diamonds from other rocks and soil. Anything about diamonds still interested her. She wondered if Isaac had been able to find his way back to his family, whether he had returned to his job in Johannesburg.

Mostly, though, her aunts would call her hence and give her some dull work to do, darning or mending or working endlessly in cross-stitch in a dull blue on a tablecloth for their dining room. She was never given white wool or a baby pattern to knit, and she had no money to buy anything of her own. She was precluded from adding to the family finances, as she could not go out to pin hems or alter dresses as she and her sisters had done at home to help. She was dependent on the good will of her aunts and had to endure the work they provided, knitting or embroidering endlessly in the dark, airless lounge, longing only to escape.

During her stay in Kimberley, no one came to visit, and if someone inadvertently rang the doorbell, Bill was told to go to her room. She was never allowed to accompany the aunts on their social visits, or even to go to church after the first few months. Sunday mornings were the only times she was left in the house alone with the door locked and the windows closed, as if she might run away.

As her time drew nearer, she became increasingly fearful. She had only a vague idea of what the birth of a baby involved, and her lack of information made her even more terrified. One morning at breakfast, she dared to ask Aunt Maud if a doctor or a midwife would be available, in case of need.

"It is surely not necessary to explain why not," Aunt Maud said severely without looking at her, concentrating on spooning her bland porridge between her thin lips.

"How will I manage on my own?" Bill asked.

"You seem to have managed very well on your own up until now, my dear. I presume you'll manage this, too," she was told.

"I might die," Bill said, in desperation, looking from one aunt to the next, as she had done that evening when she and Isaac had arrived in the house. None of them would look her back in the eye. They continued to eat their porridge in silence until Aunt Winnie said, "What a terrible thing to say. You have always been a healthy child, Bill."

"But I might!" she said, weeping. She had heard of women dying in childbirth, read of it in books; in fact, it was mainly that possibility she had heard about, that or the death of the child.

"Plenty of women have done this on their own. You won't be the first," Aunt May said, scraping her plate for the last drops of porridge. She added more kindly, "Besides, we will be here, Bill, and so will Gladys."

Clearly, the women had discussed this and come to the same conclusion. The three of them always seemed to concur, at least where Bill was concerned. It was this implacable tri-umvirate that was so difficult to countenance. Bill wanted to say that it might be dangerous for the baby, but realized that this was not her aunts' primary concern.

Sometimes, unable to sleep at night, she would slip down the corridor and go out the back door and walk a way alone in the dawn streets, even going as far as Market Square. She missed her sisters and her brother, but most of all, in the dullness and hopelessness of her days, she missed Isaac, his red hair, his long legs, the smile that brightened his sad dark eyes when he caught a glimpse of her. When he looked into her eyes he saw heaven, he had said.

CHAPTER TWENTY-SIX

1956

"They loved, would have loved to have children of their own, more than diamonds, I imagine," she tells her boys sadly, speaking of the three maiden aunts. The three of them have lingered on at the dining room table talking all through the hot afternoon. "Poor women, they didn't know what to do when we arrived on their doorstep. They panicked, I suppose. I've never really blamed them for what they did," she says quite untruthfully.

"Why did you go there of all places?" Phillip asks.

Bill doesn't answer directly but simply says that the marriage was annulled as she was not yet of age, and could not, under the law, marry without her parents' consent. She feels herself flush like a girl, wondering what else to say. Her boys are waiting for more.

After all these years she still feels ashamed of this story, though her boys do not react to it in that way. It all sounds romantic to them, but they do not know the rest and she cannot tell them, though they smile at her encouragingly. They like this story which sounds similar to the ones in their books. What more can she tell them? How can a mother speak to her children of passion? How can she speak of the consequences of her reckless actions? How can they understand the way society was structured in those days, the extreme importance of what was thought of as a woman's virtue?

"Didn't you love Father at all, then?" Mark asks her now, in a low voice, staring at Bill, as if he is seeing her for the first time. "Why did you marry him?" Bill sips from her froth-topped glass of South African beer to give herself courage, as Helen had often advised.

Isaac was, Bill admits, her hands on her chest, the love of her life. She adds quickly that she did love their father, that they loved one another very much. Certainly, she was grateful to him, and her love grew out of her gratitude. He was very good to her, to their boys, whom he loved so much.

She is moved now to say, "Poor man, he had the heart of a racehorse: fast but delicate. He had had such a hard childhood. Had to walk miles to school without shoes." This story may not be true, but she prefers to see her husband as a poor boy, walking without shoes across the veld in the pale winter light of dawn, dressed only in shorts and a jersey, his head shaved against the ringworm or later coming bravely up to Johannesburg in the *highveld* from the coast, on his own as a young man, to start his own firm, carrying the timber on his bare back. "Such a brilliant man," she says, sure of that. "Like you boys, exceptionally good at maths."

Whatever actually happened in his childhood, she is convinced her husband was a brilliant man, who could add, subtract, multiply, and divide huge numbers in his head. He had told his people in his office that they could get an adding machine when it could add faster than he could, this of course during the thirties and forties.

What would her boys think of her if they were to know all about her past? What would they do if she were to tell them what had really happened with their own father? Would they turn against her then?

CHAPTER TWENTY-SEVEN

1936

"MAKE HIM PAY FOR IT, THEN," CHARLES ADVISED. "DON'T LET him have his way with you on the sly. Make him put the ring on your finger first. Tell him you are no whore."

She told him how the husband had pursued her, coming to her in the garden, pressing against her in the corridors, or even coming into her room at night. He would open the door and just stand there, breathing heavily, cigar in hand, while she pretended to sleep.

She was aware of the irony of the situation, his wife now reduced to begging and weeping: "Whose side are you on, in the end?" she would say, banging her fist down on the table at luncheon, so that the tall Zulu who was serving would stare down at Bill angrily.

She felt all the servants in the house hated her role. She was the usurper, the one who had come into the house and taken over the Zulu's position, taken over the keys from the rightful mistress. The servants, too, were aware, surely, of what was happening with their master, who hunted her down immediately when he came back in the evenings, pushing her up against the wall in the corridor, his hands on her body.

She had threatened to leave, but then the couple invited her to go to Europe and Scandinavia with them.

They left from Cape Town, sailing on a luxury liner with streamers and a crowd of people shouting, "Bon voyage!" from the quai, and her family craning their necks to observe her, enviously, as the ship drew away. She had her own beautiful cabin with an outside window, and on a table a big basket of fresh fruit under cellophane wrapping, with a big orange bow.

Despite the disturbing news from Europe at the time, how could she refuse, when the places she had dreamed of, London, Rome, Venice, Paris, and even Copenhagen, were suddenly thrust before her? They stayed in first-class hotels and were driven around by a chauffeur in a limousine to visit the chateaux de la Loire, the great cathedral of Chartres. How could she refuse to go shopping with Helen on the Faubourg Saint Honoré to buy Parisian frocks in shantung? "Go on, it looks gorgeous on you," Helen would say. How could she resist strolling through the Tuileries on a spring day—it was spring in Europe in April—Helen on her arm, the sun coming and going, the leaves fluttering like her heart?

"Take a good look at these sights; you may never see them again," the husband said, as they went beneath a bridge on a boat lit up with garlands of lights on the Seine, slipping his hand around her waist, pulling her against his hard strong body, making her tremble, as Helen put her hand on her shoulder. He put his arm around both their shoulders on the Place Vendôme, for a photo. She still has it, with the husband looking cheerful, smug, and satisfied in a double-breasted suit, his hat at a jaunty angle; Helen in a smart hat, looking slim and elegant; and she herself, waving a large white handkerchief, as if surrendering.

It was after they had come back that she slipped quietly down the stairs one evening after dinner and knocked on the husband's study door. As usual he was working late. She approached him and said, "I have to talk to you. This can't go on. She's my friend. I can't go on lying to her like this. It's so demeaning to both of us. You'll have to find someone else. I'll have to go."

He stared at her for only a moment and then said, without any hesitation, "Alright, then, just give her what she wants. I don't care anymore."

"You mean the keys?" she asked, and he nodded his head, looking into her eyes with longing. She turned, ran up the stairs, and walked directly into the master bedroom without knocking.

Helen lay on her bed, her head propped up with pillows, reading a book. The dogs lifted their heads as she came into the room, ears pricked. "Here," she said, unhooking the keys from her belt and holding them out to her. Helen looked up from her pages—she was reading *Hard Times*. She sat up on the edge of the bed, her feet bare. She hesitated, as Bill had herself the first time the husband pressed the keys into her hand. She stared at Bill incredulously and inquired, "All of them?" Bill took her hand and pressed the ring of keys into Helen's palm, closing her long white fingers on the keys, aware—or was she?—of what would happen in the end. Helen rose from the bed, threw her arms around Bill, kissed her hard on the mouth, exclaiming, "I knew you could convince him." She put on her shoes, took Bill by the hand, and led her down the stairs to the dining room, switching on the light.

She found the key she wanted quite easily and unlocked the corner cupboard, a scent like incense filling the room, so that it seemed the cupboard had once been in a church. She took out a bottle of fine French champagne from the well-stocked shelves. She called John to bring three glasses to celebrate what she obviously thought of as her victory. She lifted her glass high. She smiled and told them both to drink up, ordering the cook to drink his though he protested, said he didn't drink alcohol. Then she gave him back the keys, all but one.

Bill drank all the warm champagne in her glass fast and then a second one. It went to her head—she was not used to alcohol then, and the whole room and the garden in the moonlight spun around her, all the shadowy flowers, the great green lawns, the trees, Helen's lovely, flushed, triumphant face.

CHAPTER TWENTY-EIGHT

✢

1936

THEN THERE WAS COMPLETE CALM IN THE HOUSE. THE COOK, now in possession of the house keys, could dole out the supplies to the servants in the mornings: the mealie meal, the flour, the "boys' meat," as he had once done before Bill arrived. Though he was far more parsimonious than she had ever been, the servants seemed happier, satisfied, things were as they should be; the rightful order in the house was reestablished. The old madam, the real one, was back in control. She herself, with the one key she needed, seemed more relaxed, more beautiful, and even more generous than before.

For his part the husband was more openly amorous, rushing home early from work and pouring out the drinks liberally, on the verandah, kissing each of them in turn on the mouth, even saying, "How are my girls tonight?" Helen didn't seem to mind. She seemed glad of his attentions to Bill, the pleasant atmosphere in the house, his elevated and more generous spirits. She enjoyed her newly acquired freedom, went off in the car into town in the afternoons to meet her old artistic friends in local bars, coming back smelling of alcohol and smoke. She took out her old typewriter and started writing a story about two women, about friendship. Happily, Bill heard her clacking away at the keys. She went away for a few days to visit her son in the Cape, leaving Bill alone with her husband, with Mark.

Now he would linger on at the dining room table after dinner, to drink port wine with both of them, telling them amusing stories about his youth, his Bavarian father who was a carpenter, who came from Kempden, a small town near Munich, about his many brothers, one of whom, Hans, had fought on the German side during the first world war. They laughed about his parsimonious mother who carried her money in a money-belt underneath her voluminous skirts on the train.

There was an endless round of parties, all through the dry winter months: big cocktail parties in the evening on the glassed-in verandah with champagne and caviar and laughter in the air; luncheon parties with ladies from the neighborhood in pretty hats and gloves, with potted shrimp and eggs à la russe, everyone flushed with wine and loquacious; tea parties in the garden on the warm afternoons with cucumber and smoked salmon sandwiches and scones, and the silver teapot beautifully shiny and everyone tipsy on sweet sherry. At every party, Bill was warmly introduced as the best friend, the indispensable companion, the darling girl. Though the women eyed her suspiciously, and the men squeezed her arms and pressed up against her in the dark, for a while she thought it was fine, fine, fine. It was all perfect. Charles had been right. The husband had exaggerated the problem. Helen would be alright, and so would she.

CHAPTER TWENTY-NINE

1936

She felt obliged to allow certain furtive caresses: to let the husband, Mark, reach down the front of her dress and caress her full breasts, while he pressed his lips against hers, his body against her; to touch the inside of her white thigh, to press her hand against his swelling sex.

She did not want to lose her lucrative position. She had become accustomed to luxury in her life, and her family, too, had become accustomed to the luxury she brought into theirs: new dresses for her sisters, flowers for her mother brought from the garden on her Sunday off, a pretty new scarf, or even a brooch. She contributed to the family's upkeep and to the servant's wages. They had even hired an older woman who was more efficient to help. Her father somehow managed not to see these things or made some comment on the generosity of her "companion."

Indeed, she had come to enjoy Helen's company and Mark's wit, their times together, their conversations *à trois*, their camaraderie. They went on jaunts together, taking the Blue Train down to the Cape, staying at the Mount Nelson.

She even loved Helen's dogs, who followed her around devotedly and came to her in the mornings to beg for scraps from her breakfast tray. She and Helen played tennis together, giggling—Bill was never very good at it—and went for long walks with the dogs. They drank together on the verandah in the evenings now, waiting for the husband to come home in the blue light. They had become inseparable.

In some ways it seemed to her to be a perfect arrangement. She was not at all sure which one of them she wanted more or loved better.

There was no real need for her presence in the house anymore. Helen was a much more competent housekeeper than she. She had become superfluous. It was spring again, a year since her arrival. But no one suggested she leave.

Now Helen came to her room in the mornings, while Bill lolled late in her bed with the breakfast tray and a stack of magazines, smoking cigarettes compulsively. Now she brought Bill a glass of water and an Alka-Seltzer, for her headache, along with words of advice. "Have a sherry, it will give you courage," she would say if Bill were nervous before a big party.

One evening, Bill remained in her room when she heard the bell ring for dinner. In her soft gray dress, a pink rose pinned in the décolleté, diamond studs in her ears, Helen knocked and entered Bill's blue room. She sat down on the edge of the bed with a rustle, her perfume sweet, cloying: lilies and cinnamon. Bill lay there in her silk dressing gown, trying to ignore her, turning the pages of a magazine. Helen took her hand and raised her chin, looked into her eyes.

"We are waiting for you. It's dull down there without you, darling, you know. We are just sitting there in silence and staring at one another. Mark misses you."

Bill said, "Go ahead and eat. I'm not coming down. I'm not hungry," though she was eating a bunch of grapes and cheese which lay on a plate beside her on the bed and drinking a glass of red wine.

Helen said nothing for a moment. Then she spoke. "Don't be too hard on yourself—or Mark. These things happen to many men at a certain time in their lives. I don't think they can help it, quite frankly. I know you're trying to be a loyal friend, and I appreciate it, but it might be better for all of us if you would just let him have his way and get it out of his system." Bill said nothing, just glaring at Helen, thinking, why does she worry about him and not me? What does she know about my life, what it is like to be crowded together in a narrow house with my family year after year? Helen looked back at her and traced a line around the dip in Bill's silk nightgown. She stroked her neck, let her hand linger on her breast. "You are so beautiful. I can hardly blame him," she said and bent over her and kissed her on her cheek.

Bill pushed her hand away and scowled at her.

"I'm not offering myself up as the cure for someone's system," she said and turned away.

CHAPTER THIRTY

※

1956

"Then why didn't you marry Isaac after Daddy died?" Phillip asks, pushing away the table and rocking back on his chair.

"It was too late by then, he had married someone else, years before," Bill replies. She adds, "I read about it in the paper," and she looks at them, her children, the ones she has watched grow up. She is still searching their flushed, sunburned faces, their cool gray-green eyes, for signs of what she has lost, of what might have been.

She looks at her small diamond watch and tells the boys it is time for them to get ready to leave. She is glad they have to rise from the table, gather up their books, change into their uniforms, find their school caps, their ties. She says, "You'll be late if you don't hurry." She is relieved to speak of mundane things. She determines, as her father did long ago, not to bring all of this up again. She has told them all she can bring herself to tell them. She looks out the window and realizes the light is fading and her words trail away into dusk. How little she has allowed herself to say.

Yet she remembers the blue car, swerving along the dust road to Kimberley, as her pink car purrs smoothly on the tarred road and approaches the Dutch gables of the school. She thinks of Isaac, with his arm around her shoulder as her boys leave her, throwing their arms around her neck and kissing her good-bye, holding on to her, their satchels on their backs, though the matron is standing there waiting in the stone arch of the gateway with her clipboard to check them off on her list. As she watches them go, Bill hears a rumble of thunder and looks up at the clouds gathering in the sky.

As they turn to wave to their mother in the car, the first heavy drops of a sudden summer storm splash on the hood, but her boys do not seem to care about the rain. They stand side by side, waving, tall, slim, beautiful boys, their knees bare in their gray school uniforms, apparently reluctant to leave her now. They look at her with a strange glow in their gray green eyes, their heads, no doubt, full of romantic notions.

They look at her differently now. She has acquired a sheen, a glow. How odd that this secret, which she has thought of as shameful and kept from them for so many years, would make them see her in a new and more favorable light. They feel for her in her old vulnerability, her hopelessness, the sadness of the loss of her first love. They regret her early love, her dashed hopes, understand her sorrow, as they have never felt her success, a success which has brought them forth into her life.

She loves them but cannot help feeling alone. As she watches the hard December rain fall and listens to the sound of the car's windshield wipers beating back and forth, sitting alone in the back of the big car on her way home, she thinks that now she is increasingly alone. Increasingly, she longs for the oblivion only alcohol brings.

Both her parents as well as her three maiden aunts are dead now. None of them had lived to a very old age. Johannesburg society has continued to snub her over the years and since her husband's death, has shunned her completely. Apart from her boys, whom she sees so infrequently, her sisters, and her brother, whose affection she sometimes feels depends on how much she gives them, she has no one to love. She has told her boys, "Come quickly when I die before they rip the rings from my fingers."

The fate of her lost child was never discussed with anyone either before or after the birth. A silence had surrounded her pregnancy from start to finish, almost as though it had never taken place.

Gladys, who came to live with her after the death of the three maiden aunts, is probably the only one alive who knows what happened. The aunts refused to discuss the matter. "It would be better for you not to know," Aunt Maud had said firmly when Bill had asked again and again. "It will only make you sad," Aunt Winnie said.

How could she convince Gladys to tell her what she knows? She has tried and tried again over the years with no success.

It occurs to her, as the car now enters the driveway that

leads to the block of flats, that there might be a way to get Gladys to say something. If she brings up the will, surely Gladys would feel obliged to speak out. Money often speaks louder than anything else, Bill thinks. Follow the money, she thinks, not knowing then how right she is to be.

CHAPTER THIRTY-ONE

※

1926

WHEN SHE FELT THE FIRST SHARP PAIN, SHE WAS SITTING IN silence in a high-backed chair by the window, sewing. Her aunts Maud and May were on the dark horsehair sofa, and Winnie in the armchair in the corner, their steel needles clicking away, with the endless, monotonous sound she came to think of as the music of the aunts. The one standing lamp they all sewed by had been lit in the dim, shadowy lounge. There was the odor of vegetable soup in the air, the smell of genteel poverty.

She was amazed that the first pain could be this severe, and put her trembling hands to her back. "I think the baby is coming," she said.

The aunts just looked at one another, in silence, only the sound of the rain in the room, a Cape winter rain in July. Aunt Maud took off her glasses, slowly put down the gray sock she was knitting with four needles, and rose in silence. She went down the corridor and into the kitchen to tell Gladys, who took Bill by the hand. "Come along, child," she said as though she had, indeed, become a little child, being led along the corridor to her small, shuttered room with its blue and white wallpaper and the narrow iron bedstead. Gladys told her to undress and put on her nightgown, to lie down on her bed where she spread several thin towels.

"But I don't want to lie down," she said. Now that the pain had passed, she wasn't sure this was actually the baby coming. Perhaps she had eaten too many figs? Above all, she did not want to be alone.

"Stay with me, please. I'm frightened," she said, grasping at Gladys's hand. When it rained hard like this you could smell the drains at the back of the house.

"Let me just turn down the soup," Gladys said, but Bill hung on to her like a small child. "Don't go, please. The pain may come back." But Gladys, who probably had some idea how long this would last, said, "I'll be back in a second, child." She did come back after what felt like many endless minutes, but this time armed with her own knitting and a shawl for her shoulders. She sat down in the armchair in the corner of the room and again suggested that Bill undress and get into bed and rest while she could.

Bill consented to change into the blue gown she had packed nine months before, which now hung around her shoulders and gaped across her swollen stomach, but for as long as she could manage it, she paced back and forth across the old creaky floor in her slippers, wailing in terror when the pains came upon her, carrying her off to the kingdom of the damned. Sometimes, Gladys would pace beside her, taking her by the arm and holding her hand. "Don't try to talk, child," she told Bill, who wanted to tell her what she was feeling.

In the night, when her cries became too loud, Aunt Winnie came into the room, closing the door quickly behind her. She stood by the door in her old, thin flannel nightdress and folded her hands, her hair loose on her shoulders. She told Bill that she must try, for all their sakes, to stifle her cries. "It is not necessary for the entire town to know what is happening, after all, dearest," she said.

Then Bill asked again if a doctor or even a midwife could be sent for. "The pains are so bad," Bill said, "I don't think I can bear it. I need some medical help, please. A doctor could help me with the pain." She was terrified she would die here, at eighteen, shut up in this small back bedroom without any medical help.

"We cannot do that. You know that, my dear. Besides, I don't believe there is anything anyone could do. Childbirth is a painful business, anyone will tell you that," Aunt Winnie told her bluntly, her words making Bill weep. Aunt May, who had bustled into the room too, said, "Calm yourself. It would immediately be all over town, child, you know that. We are trying to protect you, but also your parents and sisters and brother, as well as ourselves," and Aunt Maud, who had now come in and stood beside her sisters, added her doleful words to the chorus. She muttered darkly, "You might have thought of this earlier."

Bill lay in the small shuttered room, alone, or with only Gladys at her side, all through the night and the next day, and the night after that, twisting back and forth in increasing pain and terror. She was certain she was dying, her baby was dying. Something was wrong. Why was it taking so long? Why would her aunts not help her?

They came into her room briefly from time to time to see if the whole thing was over, and seemed only increasingly impatient with her and the trouble she was causing them. They sighed at the sight of her with, she felt, hardly concealed disgust. "Isn't it over yet?" Aunt Maud muttered, as though Bill were a recalcitrant child who refused to comply with their wishes. "This is going on forever," Aunt May said in annoyance, pressing her palms together. They had apparently little sympathy for her sufferings and seemed to feel that what she was experiencing, she had brought upon herself by a wanton act of sinfulness.

Afterward, with age, Bill understood the women better. She realized that, having spent all their lives as maiden women, having eschewed all temptations of the flesh for the sake of one another, having refused the continuous stream of suitors sent over to them by their cousins, all of this in an effort to claim their inheritance, it was now unbearable for them to contemplate what they thought of as Bill's easy, careless, and selfish capitulation to passion.

All their former adulation for their favorite niece had turned into what she could only interpret as hate. She should, they made it clear, keep her suffering to herself. "Pull yourself together, my dear. You are making this worse than it needs to be. Try to confront this with some courage, or at least some dignity, for our sakes if not for your own," Aunt Maud told Bill when she came into her room at lunchtime the next day, hearing her screams. Obviously, she had never felt what Bill was feeling or she would not have spoken in that way.

Bill lay on the bed sweating, her hands behind her grasping the iron bars of her bed, screaming. Only Gladys, who seemed to have had some experience in the birthing business, was kind enough to sit for long hours by Bill's side, holding on to her hand, wiping the sweat from her brow, urging her to hold on, reassuring her it would be over soon. She encouraged her to push toward the end, and prevented her from rising and throwing herself from the window.

When the baby was finally born, Gladys cut the cord, wiped away the afterbirth, cleaned the baby, wrapped her in a blanket, and put her in Bill's arms. She told her she had a healthy girl.

She seemed to look up at Bill with her baby blue eyes, to see her. Bill looked down at the chubby red cheeks, felt the little fuzz of reddish hair on the top of her head, and kissed her. She opened the blanket and slipped her finger into her hand, let the tiny, tiny fingers, each one with its minuscule fingernail, grasp hers. She touched the tiny feet, each one with the perfect ten toes. She held on to her own girl, feeling her warm body in her little blue blanket against her aching breasts.

Then, Aunt Maud, followed by May and Winnie, entered the room and came over to Bill's bed against the wall. Aunt Maud bent over Bill, telling her with more kindness and concern than she had yet shown, that she must get some rest, she must be exhausted. She had suffered terribly, poor girl.

"We're so sorry," Aunt Winnie said with tears in her dark eyes.

She had been brave, Aunt May conceded, smiling at her. Now she needed to sleep. "It will be better for everyone like this," Aunt Maud said, as she gently pried the infant from her arms. Bill looked up at her three aunts, who huddled around like shades, looking down at the little girl and sadly shaking their heads.

Despite her aching breasts, her torn and bloody body, she slept and slept, all through that day and the night, as one can only sleep at eighteen. When she finally woke, at dawn, the house was ominously silent. Her breasts aching, blood seeping down her thighs, the mattress wet, hardly able to stand on her shaky legs, she still managed to climb out of her bed and stagger to the bathroom at the end of the corridor. Then she walked through the house, wildly throwing open the doors of each of the rooms, seeking her baby, calling out to her aunts who did not move in their beds. Gladys seemed to have disappeared.

She went outside into the garden, her long bloodstained nightdress trailing behind her in the early morning dew; she wandered down the street, as though she might find her baby in the gutters or on the neighbors' lawn. Finally, Gladys came rushing after her and found her sitting, crouched over in the street, her head between her knees, unable to drag herself any further in her state of weakness and despair. It was then that she had the kindness to whisper to Bill that her baby was fine, that she would be fine, she knew.

CHAPTER THIRTY-TWO

1956

THE COOK, HAVING FED THE BOYS AND SERVED THE TEA, HAS consented to take the rest of the evening off. Bill goes into the kitchen to find Gladys. The old woman sits in an armchair in a corner of the room in the half dark, mending a sock.

"Why are you sewing in the dark? You'll go blind," Bill says.

Gladys says, "Lights cost money, Madam." She has always been careful with money, trained by the frugal aunts when still a child. There is nothing like the poverty of the genteel poor, Bill thinks.

She tells Gladys they have enough money to sew with the lights on and asks her to bring some of the good nuts and olives and the bottle of the sweet sherry, too, which she knows she likes. She wants to discuss something with her. She needs advice about something and she knows Gladys never forgets what she has learned or witnessed. She quotes from her Afrikaans Bible freely and can call up just the appropriate idiom. "*Stille water diepe grond onder draai die duevel rond*," she says, looking at Bill.

When Gladys comes in with the glasses and bottle clinking in her old shaking hands, Bill rises to help her and motions to her to sit beside her in the armchair by the window. Often they have chatted in a companionable way, sewing or knitting together, as Gladys would have done with the aunts.

"I need your help now. I need you to tell me something you have never mentioned through all these years. It seems almost in another life, those days in Kimberley when you saved me, but I'm asking you now to think back. I will tell you why."

Gladys looks at her warily, her face losing its smile. She imagines the maiden aunts may have sworn this woman to secrecy or perhaps such a thing was not necessary. Certainly the aunts must have told her as little as possible.

She considers how to put the matter, which has remained unspoken for so many years. She begins, "Mr. Parks called recently, as you know. He came to me because he thinks it is time for me to make a will." She looks to see her response, but she is looking down at her work, drawing her needle in and out of an old sock, implying that this has nothing to do with her. Bill sighs, afraid she is not going to get anywhere, once again, but she continues, "I've been thinking about it this whole week. It has been worrying me. I have thought of so many things, so many people from the past, so many possibilities. Do you understand?" Gladys looks up at her.

"It is a lot of money—money that might be very helpful," Bill adds, and the old lady nods her head. She knows about penury.

"Of course, I intend to leave you a pension should I die before you," Bill assures the woman.

Gladys shakes her head, then says with conviction, "My mistresses left me what little I need, Madam, and you have given me my clothes and a fine room in your house. Besides, my life is finished. I have lived enough years and now I am tired, very tired. My bones ache. It is time for me to rest." Her skin, even the whites of her eyes, look a deathly yellow, and the frizz of hair that escapes her neat blue turban is dead-white.

Bill says, "You are probably the only one left alive who can help me find my daughter."

Gladys shakes her head and looks around the room as though the information might lie there. She says, clasping her arthritic hands firmly, "I don't know much, Madam, as I have always said. Your aunts were not women who talked about their lives, or other people's. They kept their secrets, and I knew they expected me to keep them, too."

Bill presses her, "My boys have what they need, more than they need. Now I want to do something, at last, for my girl."

Gladys sips her sherry in ladylike fashion, pinkie finger lifted in the manner of the maiden aunts, and takes up her sewing again. She looks up in silence, frowns, and bites a lip.

"Who came to the house that day while I was sleeping? You were there; perhaps you saw who took my baby away?"

Gladys looks at Bill and admits, "I was there. I served the tea and my best biscuits." Bill pours them each another glass of sherry, watches while the old woman sips. When she puts down her glass, Bill leans forward and takes the old worn hand in hers. She says, "You were kind enough to reassure me that all would be well. What made you think that? Were you just trying to be kind? Who were they?"

Gladys looks up again, disengages her hand, and bites down on an olive, clicking together the false teeth Bill has paid the dentist for. She says, "Wait a minute, Madam, maybe I can help you, after all," and gets up slowly and leaves the room quietly, still a neat woman in her gray uniform, upright, slim, and alert after a life of hard work and poverty, at eighty, or perhaps even older. Her Spartan diet—nothing but vegetables, nuts, and fruit—the hard physical labor, polishing the parquet floors down on her hands and knees in the house in Kimberley, making beds, cooking, weeding the garden, and doing all the marketing have kept her well.

Perhaps she will not return. Perhaps she has simply gone to read her Bible which she does every night, or talk to her canaries. Certainly she has always shown admirable restraint over the years, watching and waiting perhaps for this very moment. Has the old lady been planning this from the start, Bill wonders. Has she decided it is time to offer up what she knows before she dies?

Bill thinks again with sorrow of the important role of all the women in her life: the three maiden aunts, Gladys, her sisters, her mother, and Helen, of the secrets they have hidden, the silences they have kept, the lies they have told.

CHAPTER THIRTY-THREE

1936

NO MATTER HOW RUDE OR SURLY BILL BECAME, HOWEVER LATE she rose in the morning, however long she disappeared to visit her family, Mark's appetite and Helen's endless understanding grew. It amazed her that so much bad humor could be rewarded. He augmented her salary, and gave her the boxy green Chevrolet. He begged her to accept jewelry, but she refused to take it, strengthened by her brother's admonition to "Stay strong," and "to get something for yourself."

She decided the time had come. She dressed carefully in black—she knew dark colors suited her dusky skin—put on her perfume, brushed her dark curls and approached Mark's study, as she had done that first evening. She stood in the green light before his desk and insisted that he make the situation clear to his wife.

"I won't be any man's mistress," she said firmly. She was not going to make the same mistake twice.

"What will she do without us?" he asked her, putting down his cigar. "You know she's not really . . . strong."

"She doesn't have to do without us. She can stay on with us. I don't want her to go," she replied, listening to the lonely sounds of the night garden, the chirping of the crickets, the croaking of the frogs in the fish pond.

"I don't think she would want to do that," Mark said, looking down at his hands.

"Surely she will, particularly if you point out that it's what I have been doing all this time. I don't want to turn her out of the house. Why would I do that? I love her too, you know, perhaps more than you do. She's been very good to me, and I'm grateful. She doesn't seem to mind your chasing after me—she even encouraged me to give in to you. I don't think she is interested in that part of your relationship. We can keep on taking care of her and see that she comes to no harm."

At first Bill thought her suggestion, surely, had been ignored, but a week later, as the two women already sat uneasily at the dinner table in silence, sipping their green pea soup, he strode in. Before he said anything, she realized what was coming, and her heart beat hard. She wondered if she could go through with it, if she really wanted to be Mark's wife. What would Helen say? How could she take her place?

He was dressed in an elegant gray suit, hand stitching on the lapels, a pale pink shirt. His black shoes shone with a hard dull glint. As he strode purposefully toward them Bill could smell his eau de cologne. He took his seat at the head of his shiny mahogany table and turned to his wife. He said, in his low, firm, and persuasive voice, "I have a proposition to make to you, darling."

"And what is that?" Helen asked, looking from Mark to Bill, who could only lower her gaze.

Mark began by apologizing to her, saying he knew he had been autocratic, demanding too much of her, and never giving her sufficient freedom. He had made her do things she hadn't wanted to do, and here he lowered his gaze, fiddled with his spoon, waved away the soup John was trying to serve him. He said he had tried to do his duty but that had not been her pleasure. He looked at her, and it was now she who lowered her gaze.

It was time to change all of that, he said, taking up a contrite air. He wanted to make amends. If he could do it all over again, he would do it differently, he said, but we cannot change the past, only the future.

"And how do you suggest we do that?" Helen asked warily.

"I have thought of an arrangement that might suit everyone better—not much of a change at that, just a little more open and honest, with something in it for each of us," he said, becoming more cheerful.

"I'm sure you have," Helen replied, looking from him to Bill. "Go on."

Bill now wanted only to stop this declaration, or to delay the moment. She said, "Perhaps you two should discuss this on your own, in private."

But Mark shook his head. "We are all friends here, and

I hope we will remain friends. No more secrets in this house. No more lies," he said. With a glint of mischief and his naughty-boy grin, he plunged ahead:

"You get your freedom, all the keys, the control of the servants, and the best room in the house. I get what I want, and Bill gets to be an honest woman."

CHAPTER THIRTY-FOUR

✻

1936

As soon as Helen had signed the divorce papers, the civil ceremony and then a small reception was held on the lawn at the house. A photographer took a photo of Bill and Mark standing on the lawn, Mark's arm around her shoulders. She is wearing a wedding outfit which always puzzled her boys: a smart brown suit. No orange blossom, no long white dress, and no veil. Her dark hair is parted in the middle, and she holds a bunch of white roses, this time, in her hands. Her sisters are the bridesmaids, wearing beige, and Charles, as the best man, grinning widely, appropriately holds the large blue white diamond Bill will wear as a wedding ring.

Helen, who was spared this ceremony, went away to visit her boy at his boarding school in the Cape while Mark and Bill were on their European honeymoon.

Before Helen's return, Bill carefully prepared the big blue room as Helen had once done so carefully for her. She, too, filled the vase with roses from the rose garden, laid out an initialed dressing gown and fresh towels and a new cake of French soap in the bathroom.

She was waiting in the hall to welcome her back home when she heard the car drive up.

She had already begun to find the days alone with Mark long and hard to fill. Now that he was no longer courting her, he reverted to being self-absorbed, and to finding her chatter tiresome. He was an active man, whose pleasure lay in his work.

"Darling, I'm so glad you came back. I missed you," she said quite truthfully to Helen, kissing her pale cheek warmly. Helen said nothing and went up to her room, followed by her dogs, her expression sly and cold. What else could she do? Where else could she go?

But she came down for dinner at eight, looking elegant in a new gray chiffon dress. The three of them ate together in the long dining room, almost as though nothing had changed. Mark sat at the head of the table, content with the two women on each side of him, making polite conversation, John bringing in the dishes in better humor than he had shown since the wedding. "Just like old times," Helen said.

But there were no more dinner parties. Even her Bohemian friends found Helen's decision incomprehensible and refused to come to the house. They considered the threesome too strange. Thus their dinners became increasingly intimate, the silences increasingly long and loaded.

Both women drank in larger and larger amounts, and after several bottles of wine, smoldering resentments inevitably surfaced.

Helen had lost weight and looked somewhat gaunt. She filled Bill's empty glass and watched her drink it down thirstily. Then she said, with a hint of irony in her educated voice, and a slightly smug smile, staring at Bill, in her elegant black dress and her large diamond ring, "It's remarkable, darling, isn't it?"

"What is remarkable?" Bill asked warily.

"I seem to have taught you to enjoy your liquor as much as I do. Soon poor Mark will have to hire a companion to take the keys and watch over you!"

"How dare you talk to me like that," Bill said. But it was Mark who really lost his temper, bringing his fist down and shattering a good Wedgwood plate. "I expect peace in my household. I've had a long day at work," he said looking from one woman to the next.

At this manifestation of bad humor, Helen simply got up and left the table, floating toward the door, her linen napkin in hand, as she had done that first night Bill had come into her home.

CHAPTER THIRTY-FIVE

1936

HELEN WAS LESS AND LESS ABLE TO PLAY THE GAME. SHE DE-
clined to come down for meals, taking them in her room,
which she rarely left, preferring to spend her time reading
her French and Russian books, writing at her desk, or complaining on the telephone to her son or those few friends
who remained. She came out only to walk her dogs, and
after a while, she had Bill do even that for her. The kidney-
shaped basket was moved back into a corner of the master
bedroom. John became the only one she would speak to
with civility, in Zulu.

Bill still went to see her each morning, as she had done
at the start of her stay in the house. She attempted, as she had
done before, to distract her. Helen looked increasingly thin,
her skin yellowed, her legs like brittle twigs, as she sat up in
bed with her moth-eaten pink cardigan around her shoulders, her gray hair unbrushed and caught up with a comb on
the top of her head. "Go to your man, your precious husband, the one you have stolen from me!" she rasped.

It became increasingly apparent that she was seriously ill, but she refused to see a doctor. The only ones whom Helen consented to have at her bedside as she lay smoking and drinking were John and her boy, a skinny, blond seventeen-year-old, who appeared in his short gray pants, his knees bare, summoned from his boarding school to sit weeping at his mother's side.

WHEN JOHN CAME TO CALL Bill one morning early, standing solemnly before her, his head bowed, saying, "You better come quickly," she went at once into Helen's room. Bill found her alone, having difficulty breathing. Her boy had left the room, stepping out into the garden, leaving the windows open, perhaps after a sleepless night. Bill shut the window and was about to call a doctor when Helen sat up in her bed and reached out to her. "Hold me, please," she said. Bill caught her up, pressed her to her breast, and held her tightly as she slipped away without a sigh, her head falling onto her shoulder lightly, going away as easily as she had come to her that first day, walking down the steps of the lounge, her face settling back into all its spring sweetness. Bill lay her down against the damp, stained sheet, seeing her pale, placid face as it was when she had first taken her hand and led her out into the spring garden she had made so beautiful.

Bill stayed by her side until they came to carry her away. Then she stayed there alone, the room so empty, it felt empty of her, too, as though she had gone with Helen.

Though Bill had known she was ill, she had not expected this, not now, not this morning, the sun shining, the garden in all its glorious bloom, her piano open in the lounge, her music books still on the stand, waiting for her.

On the day of the funeral Bill wandered around the blue room in her petticoat, as though she could still find Helen there. She was remembering the day she had got her dressed and downstairs and put on a record and danced with her, the windows open on the garden.

Mark paced back and forth. His cheek twitched. She put her hand to it to still the muscle. He brushed it away. "Get yourself dressed and come downstairs. You must put in an appearance. You think this is easy for me!" he said, turning on his heel and leaving the room.

John, his impeccable starched white uniform with a deep black sash across his chest, passed around champagne and canapés. People in dark clothes whispered in small groups, their heads close, commenting on the strange choice of refreshments and glancing at Bill sideways with disdain as she crossed the room. No one came up to her. She stood against the wall alone, moving her mouth, thinking of Helen, and feeling cold in the warm room.

Many of the servants left after that, too. Bill was left increasingly alone in the big house, only alcohol to fill the emptiness, as she is this afternoon, sipping sweet sherry, after leaving her boys at their boarding school, waiting for Gladys in the faint gray light, listening to the sounds of the growing storm.

CHAPTER THIRTY-SIX

1956

BILL HEARS GLADYS'S SLOW, SHUFFLING FOOTSTEPS AND HER panting in the corridor. She comes back with something in her gnarled, trembling hands. "I looked everywhere. I'd put it in an old sweets tin on top of the cupboard, and I'd forgotten about it. But here it is," she says. She lets Bill take the small blue book from her. Bill smoothes the soft leather cover, carefully hand-stitched around the edges. She recognizes it immediately, with a rush of all the emotion she had felt during those nine months in her aunts' house in Kimberley: the address book, which was always left in the hall beside the telephone, which she was forbidden to use.

How often she had looked at the telephone with longing. What would have happened if she had told Isaac he was to be a father? She is certain now that the boy, young as he was, would have come to fetch his own child, and her lack of courage, her poor estimation of herself at seventeen, saddens her more than anything. Somehow that triumvirate of aunts, with their disapproving stares, clacking needles, and upright backs, had silenced her completely.

Gladys looks at her mistress with her steady, bright gaze and says, "I kept it as a souvenir of the good ladies. They did their best for you, you know, Madam. They wept bitter tears." Bill nods her head at the old cliché, though she is not at all sure it is true.

"Come and sit by me," she says, patting the pink chintz on the sofa beside her and telling Gladys to help herself to another glass of sherry, while outside the wind continues to blow and the rain spatters against the windows. She opens the little address book, looking at the few neat names, filled with sadness to see in the aunts' small circle of acquaintances and friends this record of their circumscribed lives all written in Aunt Maud's neat handwriting in royal blue ink.

"Perhaps there is something in there," Gladys suggests, looking down at the pages, keen-eyed, though Bill knows she has never learned to read, though she managed that day to sign her name so bravely for them.

Gladys takes Bill's hand as she says, "I know the good ladies did not want me to say anything to you. They thought it would just add to your suffering, you see, but now, perhaps, they would understand. She was such a beautiful baby."

Bill nods, tears falling down her face, taking out her handkerchief from her sleeve. She is overcome at these words, spoken so simply after so many years of silence. "Tell me what happened to her. Tell me what you know."

"It was a woman who came to take her," Gladys confesses as Bill looks under the A's for adoption agencies in the telephone book but finds nothing there.

"You actually met her?" Bill asks.

"Of course I was not introduced, Madam—though I did hear her name spoken a few times before the baby was born and on that day. She visited to talk things over with your aunts, when they were trying to decide what to do with the baby, but it was such a long time ago."

"More than thirty years," Bill says. "Did you catch a glimpse of her? Do you remember what she looked like?"

"I never forget a face and particularly not that one, Madam. I made the lady a cup of tea and brought her my good biscuits."

"So you did see her clearly," Bill says.

"She seemed a nice, neat lady. I remember her quite well. I gave her a good look. I wanted to make sure she looked alright, Madam, you understand."

"And what would you have done if she hadn't?" Bill cannot but ask in a hard voice, her old anger resurfacing suddenly at the thought of this betrayal. "Would you have woken me? Warned me?"

Gladys just looks down at her old hands and then up at Bill. Perhaps she does not know the answer to that question. Perhaps she is thinking it is a question she has asked herself many times, and that Bill has no right to ask her. She simply says, "My mistresses were very poor. You don't understand, perhaps. Their money had run out. They hadn't paid me for years. I couldn't abandon them. What would they have done?"

It occurs to Bill then with a flash of knowledge what must have happened. Why has she not thought of this before? "You knew and didn't let me know they were going to sell my baby!"

Bill looks at Gladys and realizes she has never had any idea of what the woman actually thought at the time. Gladys goes on, "I remember the clean white gloves and the polished shoes. I notice those things. You can tell a lot about a lady from her gloves."

"Go on," Bill says, afraid the old woman, who is in her own way a terrible snob, will lose the thread of her thought, and instead give her a sermon on the qualities which constitute a lady, which she seems to suspect Bill might be lacking.

"Not a smart lady—her clothes were not new, I could see that, but she was neat enough, and she did what she said she would."

"You mean she paid up?"

Gladys goes on, "I watched the way she held the child—properly—when she took her from me in the hall."

"You were the one who put her in the lady's hands?" Bill asks, feeling tears coming again. She wants to ask her, "Why didn't you come and wake me? Did they pay you off, too?"

Gladys purses her lips. "Well," she says, "your aunts didn't want to touch the baby! When they took her from you, while you were sleeping so soundly, they brought her to me and I gave her some sugar-water when she cried and walked her up and down in the kitchen. I put my finger into her mouth to suck. When the lady had drunk her tea, the aunts called me into the lounge. They told me to bring in the baby, who was sleeping so sweetly by then. The lady wanted to look her over. I had to unwrap her, let the woman see her fingers and toes."

Bill cannot help asking, "And why didn't you come and

wake me then? You must have known how desperate I would be."

Gladys looks down at her hands and says, "When we were standing in the hall, and I put the baby into her arms, I did ask if they didn't want to wake you, so you could say good-bye. But they all just looked at me, Madam, as if I was mad. And I thought, why make you suffer more. I thought, perhaps it was better for both, in the end."

"No one mentioned the name of the people who were buying my baby?"

Gladys shakes her head. She continues, "Perhaps if you read me the names in the address book, I might recall the name of the lady. It was a curious one. I knew all of the people who came to the house, and she wasn't one of them," Gladys says, drawing herself up proudly and looking across the room as though the people were coming in for tea.

"I'm sure you knew them all well," Bill interrupts, hoping to get the old lady back to her story but thinking too that these people Gladys is proud to have known by name must only have known her as Gladys, or sometimes just the girl. Bill thinks of this intelligent, sensible, and perceptive woman's long life of servitude, of the waste of time and talent.

She proceeds to do as Gladys suggests. There are so few names. She reads them all slowly, looking up at Gladys after each one. When she reads, "Mrs. S. McNulty," Gladys puts her hand on Bill's wrist. She says that may have been the one. "I remember thinking it had a sound like a nut," she says.

"Hard. A hard job she had, buying babies and taking them from their mothers," Bill says, and looks at Gladys. There is a telephone number and an address.

"Thank you, Gladys," she says. "I'm so very grateful for this," she adds, holding the blue address book to her knocking heart.

The woman is probably dead by now, Bill thinks, or will have retired, but through her or someone who knew her she will be able to find the child. "You have kept this all these years," she says and wonders if Gladys realized all along it must contain the name she wanted so badly. There is not much Gladys does not know.

CHAPTER THIRTY-SEVEN

※

1926

FIVE DAYS AFTER GIVING BIRTH, SHE STOOD ALONE IN THE lounge of the house in Kimberley, waiting for her older sister and little brother. Her parents had sent them together on the train to bring her back home. She watched out of the window, lifting the net curtain as her aunts had done nine months before. She saw her little brother approaching and walked quickly into the hall and threw open the front door as he came running fast to her in his short gray pants. He threw his arms around her waist, in that dark hallway with its hat stand and smell of floor polish and wax. She recalls how his words, his body against her aching one, comforted her. "I missed you so much," he said, burying his head in her lap.

"I missed you, too," she said and wept for him and for what she had lost. He was eight years old. He told her that he had insisted on accompanying Pie, who was nineteen by then, a tall, thin, gangly girl, who hugged Bill tightly to her chest. "We all missed you," she said.

They helped her close her small cardboard suitcase with

her few belongings and led her down the corridor. In the hall the three aunts stood in silence in a row in order of age. She could not bring herself to kiss them good-bye or to thank them for taking her into their home, though she realized they had done what they considered their duty at some cost to themselves. She glanced at them angrily, reproach in her eyes. Their silence about her child still infuriated her, though since the birth they had treated her kindly enough, bringing her more copious meals than she had ever had in that house, telling her to stay in her bed and rest, encouraging her to eat and regain her strength, and even having Gladys mend, wash, and iron her clothes.

Many years later, she would see them again. At Christmas, when she was married again, she would send them a gift every year, sending them the very things she had so craved as a pregnant girl in their house: a large Christmas cake, jars of jam and marmalade, and bottles of port wine.

Later, she was able to think of them more kindly, but at that moment, standing in the hall where she had been so unhappy, she hated them with all her heart. They had stolen her child, snatched her from her aching body. She would have left them standing there in silence, but Aunt Winnie grasped her by the hand, leaned forward, and brushed her chapped lips against her cheek. She said, "Don't think too badly of us, child. We have done our best."

At the station café, the three of them ate a large breakfast of eggs and bacon, sitting in the sunlight, before boarding the train. They gave her the best bunk under the window where she wept with the sound of the train wheels going round and round, going away from the place where she had been so briefly happy, from her baby who was all that was left to her. Charles came and lay beside her as he had done so often.

There was the sound of the train moving and a sudden whistle as it came to a stop. There was complete silence in the empty, dry veld, dust in her mouth.

CHAPTER THIRTY-EIGHT

❋

1926

ON HER ARRIVAL HOME, SHE DECIDED SHE WANTED TO NURSE the sick and the disabled, to help the suffering, others in need. Together, she and a friend went off on their own to nursing school. She had her photo taken in her uniform, smiling, her hand to her cap in the wind, two other nurses next to her, sitting on a wall. It is a photo she would always keep, and her boys would one day find. With some diligence Bill applied herself to the practical studies which interested her, for once.

One week later her father arrived in the hall at the nursing school and asked for her.

"What are you thinking! Girls who become nurses are the lowest of the low," he told her. "You'll be nothing better than a skivvy, my girl. I'm not having any daughter of mine wiping the bottoms of the very poor." This time she didn't listen to his old tired words and she stayed on and finished the one-year course.

She never talked about what had happened, though she

thought people probably knew her story, but never confronted her. It was never alluded to. A silence spread around her, seeping into everything and above all amongst her own family, her brother, her sisters, her parents.

"We will not speak of this again, ever, do you understand," her father had said that day in Kimberley, and he never had until the day of his death. Neither of her parents had lived very long lives. They did not see her give birth to either of her boys. Her father had had a weak heart and had always worked too hard, coming back late at night and leaving early each morning and having to cope with a household of children, which her mother was not able to do.

It was not until Bill herself decided to speak of her love affair with her children that something was said and even then she told so little of the truth.

CHAPTER THIRTY-NINE

1956

SHE DOES NOT KNOW WHAT MR. PARKS KNOWS ABOUT THE matter, but surely with the name of the woman who took her baby she will find her. There must surely be some record of the child's existence somewhere. If she can bring herself to speak of this secret matter, if she has the courage, she will find her child.

Taking a deep breath to steady herself, she telephones Mr. Parks.

"Good evening," he says. "Quite a storm we have raging."

She has no desire to talk about the weather. "I've done as you suggested and given this matter serious thought, and I'm ready to make my will," she tells him.

"I'm so glad to hear that, my dear. I think it may be wise," he says.

She listens to the sound of the rain, which has turned to hail. A brutal summer storm. "You can come whenever you wish. You could even come tonight, if you're willing to face the elements," she says.

A little over a half hour later he is in her lounge again, looking pink in the face. This time she is dressed appropriately in a dark silk dress. She wears her rings on her fingers, and pearl earrings dangle from her ears. She ushers him inside herself and offers him a gin and tonic. She thanks him for his advice, tells him it has been helpful. It has set her thinking.

"I'm glad if anything I said was helpful," he says a little smugly, already annoying her, seated once again in her living room in his shiny gray suit with the padded shoulders.

"Yes, well, I realize you think I should leave the money to my boys, but I have some other ideas."

"It is entirely up to you, my dear, of course. It is your money," Mr. Parks says disapprovingly, looking at her and stroking his mustache. He puts his drink down and takes out a notebook and black fountain pen, removes the top, and starts writing something down.

"Indeed," she says.

She decides then that she will do as she pleases for once in her life. Surely, Mark would understand, and if he could not, he should. She will leave her sisters something and her brother a bit more, she tells Mr. Parks, one million between the three of them. She doesn't care whether they consider it sufficient. She will reward Whit, too, for a pleasant evening, for amusing her, whatever his motivation. Indeed, she'd like to spend some time with him. Why not? Perhaps she'll even make a trip abroad with him. She has always wanted to go back to Italy and swim in the Mediterranean Sea, back to some of the places she visited with Mark and Helen. Now she will do it again and with a charming companion of her own choice. She adds, "I'd like to leave something to Pie's nephew."

"Pie's nephew?" he says, looking confused, lifting his pen from the page.

"Yes, her sister-in-law's child, the young actor, Whit Johnson, such a nice young man."

"Is that wise?" Mr. Parks asks doubtfully, putting down his pen and folding his hands in his lap.

"I want to leave him a small sum of money—perhaps two or three hundred thousand pounds, with the capital going to my boys when he dies, which will allow him only to touch the income generated, do you see?"

"Yes, I do. Well, of course, that sounds wiser, and I will respect your wishes, if you insist," Mr. Parks says and takes up his pen again.

"I do insist. Make a note of it. And I haven't finished. I'd also like to leave a similar amount to John," Bill says, thinking of the old man who has taken care of them all these years. "He's been so good to my boys."

"John, the native boy?" Mr. Parks asks.

"He's an old and dignified man, who has worked much of his life for me, as has Gladys," Bill says.

"Your husband provided John with a small pension, I believe, as your aunts did for Gladys," Mr. Parks says.

"I know, but I'd like to add to it."

"As you wish, though I imagine they will both die well before you, my dear," Mr. Parks says with a smile, and Bill cannot help smiling at the tone of his voice, the disappointment on his face. Obviously this is not what he had in mind, this long list of people who will receive money at her death, is perhaps not at all to his liking, though he writes down their names.

"But all of this doesn't add up to much," he interjects. "What about the rest of your fortune?"

CHAPTER FORTY

🌿

1936–1946

JOHN WAS ONLY PERSUADED TO STAY ON AFTER HELEN'S DEATH when he learned Bill was expecting a child. He looked like death himself, ashen-faced and solemn, continuing with his duties in the big house punctiliously but hardly addressing a word to the new mistress, a pregnant one at that.

Though he has continued to work for Bill all these years, and is devoted to her children, his first loyalty is still to Helen. Indeed, he is always telling her with an air of digni-fied reproach, as though she were responsible, that the old madam has come to him in his dreams. He is fiercely loyal and would gladly give his life for those he loves, and above all he loves her boys.

Bill hoped that with the coming of the children, the house would fill up again with laughter, and the pall would lift. Indeed, the few remaining servants, following John's example as always, seemed to accept her more readily after it became apparent she was to become a mother.

When she returned from the hospital in her flowered hat

and long gloves, her infant boy wrapped in a magnificent white shawl, despite the warmth of the December day, she held him tightly as she climbed out of the car. He had arrived fast and easily, thanks to the administration of chloroform at the appropriate moments. Surrounded by kind nurses and efficient doctors in a proper operating room, Bill had held onto her big, blue-eyed baby boy gratefully when he was placed in her arms.

Now all the servants were lined up to greet her in the hall, smiling and clapping their hands and offering congratulations and admiration for the blond boy child. At first Bill did not notice the young, pink-cheeked woman standing amongst the other servants in her neat white nurse's uniform and cap. Mark introduced Miss Jacks, a trained Scotch nurse, he said. Smiling at Bill sweetly, with a dimple in her chin, she said, "You must be exhausted, do go and lie down," and she took the baby from her arms, telling a servant to turn the bed down for her mistress in the master bedroom and to draw the shutters.

Left alone in the darkened room with Mark, he took off her hat, her gloves, and embraced her warmly. He said how proud he was of her, and how glad he was to have her well and back home. "We must have a party to celebrate," he said, settling her down on the bed beside him. He had something for her, he added, and brought forth from his pocket a blue velvet box. "Go on, open it," he urged, as she hesitated, looking down at the box as though it might explode in her hands. She lifted the lid on a spectacular, oval-shaped sapphire ring, "As blue as our baby's eyes," he said proudly. Bill kissed him and thanked him for the beautiful ring and for hiring the trained nurse, but said she would prefer to take care of the baby herself. She could feel her milk coming down. He smiled as though she had made a lewd reference. "Then let me help you," he said and proceeded to help her undress. He suggested, leaning over her and stroking her cheek softly, that breast-feeding, for a woman in her position, was probably better confined to the hospital. He said he adored his baby boy, that he would work harder than ever to give him all the opportunities in the world, but he did not want to share her beautiful breasts with some mewling and puking infant. As he spoke he reclaimed his property, now swollen with milk, putting his hands into her lace gown and caressing her softly. Bill thought of Isaac saying "And this is mine, and this is mine."

"I need you by my side, my girl," he said, climbing up beside her and thrusting his hips against her, placing her hand on his sex, making her stroke him, bend down over him, pressing her head down to encourage her onward, to rub her lips on his sex, to suck him.

When he had finished, he put his arms around her lovingly and told her to get some rest, adding that the baby would prosper being bottle fed, and they would sleep soundly through the night.

Bill found it difficult to complain. Mark's regime was not unpleasant. She was not asked to change diapers or burp the baby, or walk the floor with a sick child in the night. The pretty pink-cheeked Scotch nurse was perfect: experienced, sensible, unfailingly cheerful, and very affectionate. Bill's sisters when they visited admired the new baby, and told Bill how well she looked, and what a lucky woman she was, not having to rise in the night with a colicky baby. The little boy was brought to Bill's bed with the breakfast tray, with the coffee and hot milk and sliced tropical fruit in the mornings.

When baby Mark was three months old and the trained nurse had left, Mark hired an English nanny, selected from an English periodical called *The Lady*, leaving Bill free to cater to her husband and her own whims, to be his partner in the work he accomplished so successfully, and to make sure she was always beautifully attired and sufficiently rested and well-groomed.

Despite their young children, Mark expected Bill to travel with him whenever and wherever and for as long as he wished. They traveled the world, going to all the places she had once dreamed of visiting. They went back to Paris and London and Copenhagen, leaving the children behind with the nanny. Bill thought of Helen's story, and how she had complained about her husband. He was obliged to travel for his business, even during the war years, going from country to country buying timber for several months. Bill suggested they take the children with them, but Mark pointed out that much as he loved their little boys, it would be selfish on their part. They needed a stable environment, a stable schedule, and they were used to their nanny now. They would be better off in the freedom of their big house and garden where they could run around barefooted in the South African sunshine and fresh air.

She enjoyed traveling, would always enjoy going to new places and seeing new sights, but still, she missed her little boys, and sent them postcard after postcard and parcels of fancy clothes and shoes. She missed Helen, too, who had been such a good companion, such an excellent guide, who spoke several languages and knew which museums to visit, which gardens to walk through, and where to shop. Sometimes Bill had to endure long, boring dinners with people she did not know who spoke about matters she did not understand. Then she thought of Helen saying, "He's impossible."

Mark, though he loved her and made sure she had anything she wanted, was, as Helen had warned, a man used to getting his own way. He had little patience after a day of hard work, and could explode unexpectedly. Above all, her husband expected her to be ready to accept his embraces at any moment of the day or night.

One hot summer night during a business trip to Europe, she sat beside him in the back of a taxi. She could see his face in profile: a heavyset man now, in his double-breasted suit, twenty years older than she, tall, bald, the glow of the Cuban cigar he was smoking lighting up his face. They were coming back from the theater in London where they had seen a Shakespeare play. Her husband liked Shakespeare. She was sleepy—it had been a long play and before that a heavy dinner and a bottle of wine. She can hardly remember which play it was at this point, though she knows it was one of the tragedies, where everyone died at the end, perhaps even *Hamlet*. She had already dozed a little during the performance, though they had excellent orchestra seats.

She was wearing a blue strapless evening gown, with a full net skirt and a bodice decorated with sequins. As the taxi turned a corner, she was thrown against Mark's chest. He stubbed out his cigar and started fumbling and pawing at her bodice and her breasts with one hand and lifting her skirt with the other. He was breathing heavily, muttering the words he liked to use at such moments, words that *he* found exciting but which couldn't have been further from the truth: "I know this is what you want, isn't it?" His thick hairy fingers searching between her thighs, pushing her legs apart, pulling her panties aside, probing. He was pushing himself up against her.

"What on earth are you doing?" she had protested, unable to believe the man could not wait until they got back to the privacy of their hotel.

"Be quiet!" he snapped, smacking away her hand. Perhaps he thought he had paid enough for her to obey him. Whatever he was thinking, he proceeded onward, caught up in the rush of his desire, straddling her uncomfortably, moaning embarrassingly—she was sure the cabbie could hear everything, each thrust of Mark's swollen member into her body, seeking satisfaction in her flesh.

CHAPTER FORTY-ONE

1946–1956

EVEN NOW, SITTING OPPOSITE MR. PARKS AND LISTENING TO the sound of the rain, she remembers her extreme embarrassment and the pricking feeling of Mark's hairy, sweating arms on her tender skin. She had wanted then only to have the act finished, and thus encouraged him onward.

On her return home eighteen months later, she entered the hall of the house with great gladness, standing in her flowered hat and long gloves, surrounded by a sea of monogrammed suitcases. She called out the children's names joyfully. "Where are my darling boys?" she said, looking up the stairs. Two thin little boys appeared at the top, staring down at her dumbly, blond white hair in their eyes. "Come and kiss me, my darlings!" she called out, opening up her arms, though they had grown so much she hardly recognized them. But they hesitated like two frightened birds on thin legs. They looked at her warily, perching on the steps in their identical blue and white sailor suits with the big collars she had sent them from Harrods. After eighteen months of absence, they hardly seemed to know who she was, until the nanny in her white uniform with her double chin came and put her hands on their shoulders, pushing them forward, telling them to go down the stairs and kiss their mother and say hello. Holding hands, they stepped slowly and diffidently down the green-carpeted stairs, in their high red lace-up shoes, making her heart ache. As she rushed to hold them she could feel their little stiff bodies draw back from her unfamiliar scent, her tight embrace.

She followed the children around as they went through their day. They would look over their shoulders at her as though she were an unwanted shadow.

The nanny, who was aptly named Miss Prior, had taught the little boys to say their prayers, morning and night, kneeling by the bed. She took them to Sunday school and read them Bible stories. She had taught them to love all of God's creatures equally, great and small. The boys, Bill realized, had taken to religion with something like a passion.

She took to drinking several beers at her lonely luncheons in the dining room of the big house when the children were at school. In the afternoons when they came home, they would shut themselves up in the vast, pale green nursery with its blackboard along one wall, installed by their father to prevent any scribbling on the walls. There they would resume the chess game they had left unfinished. They were, even at a very young age, chess champions, collecting a great number of gold cups which one of the servants had arranged on a shelf in their room though they never looked at them. "You can have the gold, I'll take the silver. I have too many gold ones," Phillip told another less gifted boy. They did their homework diligently and practiced the instruments they had learned to play. Both boys were gifted musically. Mark played the violin and Phillip the flute, in the nursery, in the afternoons, without waking their mother. When she woke with a start, her mouth dry, she would hunt for them all through the vast garden, thinking they must surely be out there, only to find them shut up in the nursery playing chess on their stomachs on the floor, or honeymoon bridge.

"Can I play with you?" she would say shyly, leaning against the jamb of the door, like an unwanted guest.

"But you don't know how to play bridge," they would say, looking up at her, distractedly, which was true. Mark had tried to teach her but she had never gotten the hang of it.

"What about Old Maid?" she would propose, hopefully.

"Boring!" they both said at once and pulled a face. Sometimes she thought there was something devilish about the way they looked at her. She would retreat, telling herself that they seemed content together, murmuring to each other, laughing softly at jokes she could not understand or share. She would shut herself in her room in the long, solitary evenings and order up a bottle of wine.

When the boys were eleven and nine, they begged to be sent away to their church school as boarders. "All the other boys are boarders," the older one said.

"But won't you miss me? Won't you be homesick?" Bill asked them, but they just gazed at her blankly. "Everyone else is a boarder, all our friends. Besides we can't *play* with you," Phillip explained bluntly.

"I would miss you too much," she said. "You are all I have in the world, my darlings," she said truthfully.

She was called in for a talk with the headmaster in his book-lined study. A thin, tall gentleman, Mr. Carnarvaron wore a black turtleneck sweater and a tweed jacket with patches on the elbows, despite the heat. He had a wart on his chin and a masters from Oxford. He greeted Bill warmly, grasping both her hands with his long cold fingers as though he knew her well. In her hat, gloves, and jewelry, she sat before him, and he smiled at her, showing yellow teeth. He said what a delight it was to have her sons as students. He gushed graciously, leaning forward to say both her boys were not only academically gifted but also diligent. "The older one particularly so. He tells me he has already read much of Rudyard Kipling!" the man said, amazed. "Is it possible?"

"Probably," Bill said sadly. "He's always reading and I know he's read *She*, as my sister read him the beginning when he was seven."

The headmaster gave Bill a puzzled look, and she wondered if she had confused the authors here. He said, "He's quite remarkable for his age and such a hard worker—up late at night and early in the morning with his books. We even found him with a torch under the covers reading after lights out! How lucky you are to have two such good, diligent children," the headmaster went on.

She said, "It has its disadvantages," and smiled, but the man looked at her blankly, asking her if she minded if he smoked his pipe, knocking the tobacco out into the ashtray.

"Actually, I do mind," she said. "The smoke makes me

sick." The headmaster put his pipe away and said he felt both boys would profit enormously from the regular life and discipline that boarding school would provide, so that their gifts could flourish.

"But I love them so much," Bill told the man, clasping her hands to her chest. "I would hate to be parted from them."

The headmaster replied, "If you really love them and have their best interest at heart, then I'm sure you, like the true mother before Solomon, will understand and want to do what will be best for them." Bill thought of her husband's words, stressing that it might be better for the children to be away at boarding school and in responsible hands. She loved them too much to hurt them in any way and felt obliged to comply. Somehow, a great distance had already grown up between her and them.

Once they arrived at boarding school, this distance did nothing but increase. One holiday, Phillip, now a good-looking slim boy of thirteen, green-eyed and smart, looked at his mother and said, "We really don't have much in common, do we?" Though Bill wept at the cruelty of the words, she could see it was true. Her boys were not interested in the things which had delighted her at their age: buying clothes; parties; or even the opposite sex. Even as adolescents, they were not much interested in their appearances.

"I don't want to look different from anyone else. They'll make fun of me. And have the chauffeur drop us off at the corner so no one sees him," Mark told her. How strange these rich, beautiful children were who wanted to look poor and even plain.

She began to long increasingly for the baby that had been taken from her, the little girl she could have dressed in smocked dresses, whose hair she would have curled, the daughter of the love of her life.

She fears her boys will run off and become missionaries or join some revolutionary group and end up in jail. They are always begging her to contribute to some charity or the other. Prompted by her enthusiastic boys, she has given generously to various funds for Easter flowers, lame horses, church-run orphanages, even the ANC, as well as cushions for the chapel pews. Both boys are particularly moved by the predicament of the black people in the country governed by a separatist government. She fears they will join the communist party or something more violent. Above all, their first love, as she and Mark have been away so much of their lives, seems to have always been for John. Their own father lived on the other side of the house, came and went when they were in their beds, and was rarely seen by them. The business world he was immersed in had no interest for them.

When her husband lay dying after a heart attack in the master bedroom of the house on Hume Road, the oxygen tank glinting in the dim light which filtered through the curtains, his face gray on the pillows, John stood by the bed, his head bowed with sorrow. Mark said, "I am leaving you something in my will, John. Don't spend it all on your wives. I'm counting on you to take care of my little ones for me. Make sure they are safe and well and that they prosper." And the old Zulu had bent down from his great height, fallen solemnly on his knees, and promised.

❧

1956

"My boys, after all, have the money their father left them directly, a sum that will pay for their education and any other exceptional expenses," Bill tells Mr. Parks, who is sipping his gin and tonic. "They are such good boys and not much interested in material things," she adds.

"They are still very young and perhaps don't yet realize the importance of money, having always had more than they need. Surely your husband would have wanted you to leave most of his money to his own children," Mr. Parks reiterates, in his prim way.

"I'd also like to leave something for you, Mr. Parks, a token of my appreciation, perhaps ten thousand pounds," Bill adds brightly, remembering Charles's words. "I'm so grateful to you for taking care of my fortune as well as you have done over these years, of arranging things for me. You have been such a loyal, honest, and helpful accountant. I'm sure Mark would have been happy and approved. I know how much he valued your services."

"That's very kind of you, I'm sure," he says, brightening. "It will be most appreciated. Of course, we will have to final-ize all of this, the exact amounts in the presence of a lawyer, you understand." Mr. Parks looks rather red in the face, and now accepts a second and generous glass of gin which Bill gets up to pour for him from the cut-glass decanter on the silver tray in the center of the room.

"Presuming, of course, that *you* outlive me," she cannot resist adding, turning to him with a little laugh and giving him his drink. He giggles appreciatively. The man is not entirely without humor. "Of course, of course, my dear," he says and takes a gulp of his drink.

"I realize that it was my boys you had in mind, as my beneficiaries, but there is one beneficiary, the main one as it happens, that I'd like you to help me find," she adds now, her voice trembling a little as she stands before him. She has kept this secret for so long it seems someone else's, no longer her own to be spoken aloud. Indeed, she is no longer quite sure all of this happened.

"Find? You want me to find someone for you?" Mr. Parks asks warily, looking somewhat taken aback, looking up at Bill. She bites her lip and looks around the room which seems too warm now.

But she says, "Yes, I'm sure you could do it. I have the name and the telephone number of someone who took her from my aunts in Kimberley where I was staying at the time—though it was thirty years ago. You will have to help me find the child's name and the whereabouts of this new beneficiary." She presses her hands together and waits to hear what he says.

"Of course, I'll do anything I can to help," he says uncertainly, and she can hear the reluctance in his voice. He clears his throat nervously. "Who is it that I am to find?"

She turns from him and walks over to the window, drawing back the curtain and listening to the rain. That night in Kimberley comes to her now with all its pain and misery. She sees her aunts with their ghastly gray knitting needles sending her off with only Gladys at her side to face the birth of a child in that back bedroom.

"Someone I want to leave the major part of my money to, you see," she says more forcefully, turning toward Mr. Parks, who is staring at her. She hesitates, puts her hands to her head, brushes back her hair from her face. She goes on and says aloud the words she has not voiced for so many years. "My first child, my own girl, a baby who was taken from me at birth. I want you to find her and make sure she gets the money and the jewelry. I should have looked for her a long time ago, if I had had the courage."

"And how am I to find this girl?" he asks. She tells him the story that Gladys has told her and gives him the name of the woman who is supposedly involved as well as her address and telephone number.

"I will do what I can," he says.

After he has left, she sits in the silence and stillness of the night. The storm has abated. In the empty rooms there is a new, haunting silence. The ghost of the girl she had once been comes to her quite clearly, a girl with so much hope and so many expectations, lifting back her head to gaze at the stars from Isaac's "chariot of fire."

PART FOUR

CHAPTER FORTY-THREE

1958

WHEN MR. PARKS, ACCOMPANIED BY THE LAWYER THIS TIME, arrives at the garden flat that evening, no one answers the doorbell. The green Dutch door, however, is ajar, so the two men enter, and stand uneasily in the well-waxed and silent hall, at the foot of the curving staircase with its white banister. They look at one another. Mr. Parks is not sure what to do, sweating a little in his heavy gray business suit in the warm December air.

"Bill, are you home?" he calls out, mopping his brow with a clean handkerchief. Though he has never been on intimate terms with his employer—indeed has never been certain that she likes him much—he calls her Bill. There is no response.

He looks at the young lawyer who shrugs his shoulders. He presumes she has once again forgotten the appointment she made and walks into the large calm living room with its heavy cream curtains drawn on the glare of southern light, the dry barren veld of the Transvaal, and the lingering heat of the day.

He goes forward into the kitchen, calling out the servants' names, but neither of them seem to be present, either, which, considering the open door, is alarming. Behind him the lawyer makes a little noise which might be a cough or a laugh.

"She definitely asked me to come this evening," Mr. Parks feels obliged to assert, as the lawyer is beginning to look impatient or perhaps slightly alarmed and would clearly prefer to leave, standing in the doorway and jangling the change in his pocket, a young man whose wife has just had a baby and who is ready to go to dinner with his family.

She had put him off for months, with various excuses, saying, "Surely, we will find the girl eventually?"

He assured her he had made all the necessary inquiries with his usual diligence, but this Mrs. McNulty, though she is alive and well, had not answered several letters or repeated telephone calls. He told her Gladys must have been mistaken, and suggested it might be wiser to give up a search based on such flimsy evidence. He suggested she revise her will as soon as possible. He had done his best, but it did not seem at all certain that the girl would be found. She continued to insist this woman must know something. She would not concede defeat. She was counting on him.

Still, he presumed she intended to follow his good advice, but the next he heard was that she had left town. Gladys informed him that her mistress had gone off on an extended cruise with, of all people, her sister's nephew, Whit Johnson—not, in his opinion, a suitable companion for her. All through the spring and winter months, he received bright postcards from her, from one European city or the next, always saying she was having a "lovely time" but never giving a return address. On arriving back home, she had eventually answered her telephone, and he had persuaded her to set up this appointment to draw up a new will with the lawyer, who now hovers uneasily in the entrance to the kitchen.

Mr. Parks stands in the large, spotless room with its gleaming counters and glass cabinets and strokes his mustache. He calls again for the servants, but neither Gladys or even John, who never seems to be far from his mistress and is always hanging about, listening to every word everyone says, appears.

"Perhaps we should just leave," the lawyer suggests, standing in the kitchen doorway looking rather nervous and making the odd coughing noise again, running his fingers through his thick blond hair. How young he looks, Mr. Parks thinks. But Mr. Parks, who has known the family well for so many years, after all, has an uneasy feeling in the orderly flat. The dead silence is disturbing.

"Something's not right," he says, shaking his head. "I'm going upstairs. You better accompany me," he tells the lawyer, who duly follows him up the steep carpeted steps onto the landing above. The two men stand dumbfounded at the open bedroom door.

Bill is in her peignoir, a red, embroidered kimono she brought back from Japan, he remembers. At the same time he takes in the rest of the scene. She lies on her back, her dark curls damp and clinging to her forehead, her arms still at her sides, her orange-painted toes bare. Her mouth is open, as if in a silent cry, as are her expressionless eyes, and it is quite clear to him from the waxy pallor and frozen strangeness of her face, which seems almost someone else's, that she is not breathing. She has slipped away.

He tells the lawyer to call a doctor and then walks over to the mahogany dressing table before the bay window and opens the drawer to feel for the lever at the back. He pulls out the Craven "A" tin from its secret place and feels its reassuring weight and heft. He opens it and sees that the jewelry is there, even the priceless yellow diamond, sparkling among the other multicolored stones. He stands still while everything in the shadowy room spins around him: her elaborate lace and bone corset with its suspenders still dangling, her silk half-petticoat, her chiffon dress, thrown on the chintz-covered chair by the bed, her handbag open on top of her dress, and the empty bottle of Scotch whiskey on the table by the bed.

Then he feels the lawyer take his arm and murmur something about sitting down. He staggers a little and collapses onto a chair, leaning forward, his head in his hands. He drinks the glass of water the lawyer brings him, the water trickling down his chin. He breathes deeply, in stunned silence, while the lawyer goes down the stairs to answer the door for the doctor.

When the doctor enters the room, he can only confirm Mr. Parks's opinion.

"Such a very young woman!" Mr. Parks exclaims, thinking she must have been ten years younger than he. "What was the cause?" he asks the doctor who indicates the whiskey bottle with a discreet glance, a tip of the head, and a purse of the lips. He suggests it has been what he calls "her lifestyle." Bill has died an early death as did his employer's first wife before her, brought on by drinking, less than two years after the making of her will.

Mr. Parks recalls her sitting erect opposite him, in that same splendid red kimono, propped up on pink pillows, her dark curls shining, saying, "I assure you I'm in perfectly good health." He thinks of her saying, "Presuming, of course, that *you* outlive me," laughing at him. He had suspected she was drinking heavily even then.

Now, as the only executor, he is obliged to call her family and read the will he has in hand, though secretly he hopes to be able to restore the inheritance to the two boys, the rightful heirs in his opinion. The boys have been summoned home for the funeral, one from boarding school and the other from the university in Paris where he is studying mathematics. Mr. Parks has been obliged to tell the elder boy he will have to pay his trip home with his own money.

As he reads the terms to the assembled family and servants in the lounge at the Melrose flat, Bill's sisters and brother, who sit together on the sofa, do not seem particularly pleased with their small share, but Gladys and John, hovering uneasily side-by-side in the doorway, beam at him, as though he were responsible for their bequests. Whit Johnson, who seems somehow to have known about his, has already left for Europe. The boys sit somberly, poor Phillip on the carpet, his chin on his knees, propped up against his brother's chair, in their dark clothes. Their lives of study will remain unchanged. They ask only if he has found the heiress, and who she might be. He shakes his head, sighs, and says he has no further information at the moment.

He carries out all the bequests as stipulated in the will, following Bill's instructions, and, indeed he is happy for the most part to do so. Certainly he is pleased to claim his own share, which he feels he has earned, and which enables him to send some money to his married daughter in England and to arrange for her to visit him in South Africa, and to buy his wife the new car she thinks fitting for their station.

He is particularly glad to give Gladys her part, too, which he feels she has earned, after all. He has always liked and admired the old woman who, unlike his wife, is also a good cook, and would slip him a tin of her shortbread biscuits or some other delicacy when he visited Bill. He helps her with the buying of one of the best houses in the colored section in Kimberley, which is where she goes finally to retire. He does not expect to hear from the devoted servant again, though he occasionally thinks of her and smiles with some satisfaction at the thought of her enjoying her prominent position in the colored world in Kimberley at her advanced age.

Six months later, he decides to make a visit to Kimberley himself to look up this McNulty woman and try one last time to question her in person, and get to the bottom of the matter. A maid ushers him in. Mrs. McNulty greets him politely enough, in her well-polished and orderly interior, with its heavy mahogany furniture, the feet in the form of lion's claws. She allows him to sit by her fireplace—it is a cold July day by then—in a comfortable beige armchair with its doilies on the armrests, and seats herself on the sofa opposite him. She even sends her maid, Nora, to bring in the tea tray.

He asks if she received his letters. She did, she says, pouring the tea from a silver teapot, but did not think it necessary to respond because she knows nothing of the matter. His employer's maid must, clearly, have been mistaken. "How could she not be, after more than thirty years—an elderly, undoubtedly uneducated woman?" she asks him, looking at him directly with small dark eyes.

When he asks her then why her name happens to be in the aunts' address book, and shows it to her in the shadows of her shuttered lounge, she holds the blue leather book at arm's length and flips fast through the pages, her red nails flashing. She purses her full purple lips and says there are many names here, after all, and that she may, like the others, have known the three maiden aunts slightly. They had, perhaps, exchanged telephone numbers. Goodness, all of this happened such a long time ago, how is a body supposed to remember? Perhaps they had met at church? She had once had tea at their house, she seems to recollect now, but naturally she knows nothing about a baby. She was married only briefly—her husband a ne'er-do-well—and never had any children herself.

She looks at him somewhat askance, pointing her strong nose at him disapprovingly, a neat woman in a clean white blouse with embroidery around the collar and a gray pleated skirt, still slim though somewhat ravaged. She says the story sounds fanciful to her, like something out of a fairy tale. The buying and selling of babies! Goodness gracious me! She is surprised an intelligent accountant would have listened to such a tall tale. She is amazed anyone put any faith in it. She suggests he try the adoption agencies, instead, rises, and ushers him politely but firmly to her door, murmuring that she hopes she will not be disturbed with this matter again.

Nor do the agencies themselves have any information for him, and he is not sure what to do next.

He is surprised to receive a call from Gladys in his office late one afternoon just as he is about to leave and go home to his wife.

"I think I have found her," Gladys says in her old shaky voice.

He knows immediately whom she is talking about. "Good heavens! Are you certain?" is all he can stutter.

"Well, you must judge for yourself," Gladys says. "I'll bring her to you." He is obliged to tell her that if she brings this woman into his office, he will need some sort of conclusive proof of her identity as the heiress.

"Of course," Gladys says, sounding offended, but Mr. Parks is not at all sure the old woman knows what he means.

CHAPTER FORTY-FOUR

※

1958

THEY ARRIVE THE FOLLOWING AFTERNOON, AND DESPITE HIS misgivings, he is obliged to receive them. Who has the old servant got hold of, or rather what imposter, perhaps, has got hold of her? he wonders as he ushers them both into his office, with his most frosty air. He stares at the young woman who accompanies Gladys, looking her up and down, and cautiously asks them to sit down in the leather armchairs before his shiny, neat desk.

The young, rather short, redheaded woman in a small straw hat with a black ribbon and short white gloves, with a hole at one fingertip, does not inspire much confidence as she sits down in her plain green dress, though her age may well be more or less that of the child's. Gladys, herself, in pale mauve from the shoes up to the flowered hat, looks splendid and rather pleased with herself.

They have apparently come straight from the station to him in a taxi, paid for by Gladys, he gathers. "Don't worry child, you will pay me back, I'm sure," Gladys is saying as she, too, sits down, a little breathlessly, carefully putting her old black wallet back in her cream handbag, and introducing him to her. Her name is Hannah Bloom.

He feels this is not a particularly auspicious beginning and cuts short the preliminaries. He turns to Gladys to ask her what has led her to believe this is the person they are seeking? Not usually as expansive, in fact he has never heard her say much, she now seems most eager to tell her tale. She draws herself up, sitting erect before him. She was not mistaken about the name in the address book, after all, she proclaims triumphantly.

"Really?" Mr. Parks says and looks at her rather doubtfully, strokes his mustache, and tells her to go on.

She explains how she met Nora, quite by chance. Touching her splendid mauve hat with all the flowers at the brim, she says she was buying a hat. Nora, besides working for Mrs. McNulty as a maid for years, is also the local hatmaker in the colored section in Kimberley—"A good one, and not expensive," Gladys says with a little smile.

When Gladys heard of her connection with Mrs. McNulty, she invited Nora to her new house for tea and a glass of sherry after church one Sunday afternoon, Gladys says rather grandly, making an elegant gesture with her gloved hands. As the afternoon wore on, Gladys questioned the woman closely, wanting, of course, to find out if she had been mistaken in the name. Unaware of what Gladys had in mind, Nora, after some initial reluctance, confirmed the story of the sale of the baby. Unlike the white people in the town, Nora knew it in intimate detail, Gladys proclaims, obviously proud of her detective work.

Indeed, there had been many babies who came and went in the house, brought in through the back door, Nora whispered to Gladys in the privacy of her lounge. Mr. Parks, though he rarely allows himself such imagining, can picture this scene: Gladys's impeccably neat and highly polished lounge with the white doilies on the arms of the chairs and the big black Bible, no doubt, in a prominent place, and the two dark-skinned elderly women, sipping sherry in a most ladylike fashion, speaking Afrikaans, and sharing white secrets.

While the two canaries, probably still called Paul and Gezina, though they would, of course, be different birds, sing in their cage, Nora explains how Mrs. McNulty, for a considerable fee, would help young white women in trouble find good homes for unwanted children or bring in a doctor to perform the necessary operation.

It was a secret and lucrative business. Mrs. McNulty is now comfortably retired. She often took money both from the young woman and from the couple who were desperate to find a child and unable to find one through the legal channels.

"She was a good businesswoman, very organized, and thorough," Gladys adds. Nora has always received her wages on time and has been treated fairly, allowed to go to church on Sunday afternoons. She would not want to cause her mistress any harm, Nora told Gladys nervously, and Gladys promised that no harm would come to the woman. "No one is going to harm her, particularly if she finally tells the truth," Mr. Parks assures her.

He tells Gladys this is all very well but asks if she has any concrete proof of this story. She smiles back at him, her false teeth gleaming large and white. She has thought of this, of course, opening up the clasp of her cream handbag with her mauve gloved hands and bringing forth a yellowed document with a flourish. She carefully smoothes it out on his desk for his perusal, pointing out the signatures at the bottom.

"How did you get this?" he asks.

She smiles a secret smile and explains. With the promise of a generous reward, and the names of the three maiden aunts, Nora had agreed to take a little look at her employer's ledger. A trusted servant, she has her own key to the house, and knows of her mistresses' comings and goings. She knew where to find the large exercise book with its hard black cover, which contained a neat and complete record of these transactions, hidden in the bottom drawer of a desk in the lounge. And she knows how to read.

The receipt for the transaction concerning the young woman was quite easily found, "borrowed," and brought to Gladys. Now she points out the first three signatures, which seem indeed to be those of the three maiden aunts. Each of them had taken the trouble to sign her name, in her careful, childish script, as though in giving their consent to the sale, as in all things, they were chained together eternally. Samuel and Sarah Bloom's signatures followed.

He now turns to Hannah and asks her if these signatures are, indeed, her parents'. She nods her head and says they seem to be, as far as she can tell. The document states that the undersigned were willing to pay two hundred pounds to Mrs. McNulty for a baby girl. At the bottom of the paper, in brackets and in small writing, Mrs. McNulty had added what was probably important information when she came to deciding on a price for this particular child, which Mr. Parks reads aloud.

Apparently the Blooms had lost a baby boy when he fell from the attic window of their house, which had since been boarded up. He was two years old. There was no explanation of how the child had gone up the stairs and clambered out the window on his own.

"Did you know about this death?" Mr. Parks asks Hannah. She shakes her head and says she didn't, but perhaps it is true, and would explain her adoptive mother's bouts of melancholy and also the curious fact that the room where she grew up was lined with blue striped wallpaper with red trains. It also, of course, Mr. Parks thinks, explains why the Blooms were probably unable to use more conventional methods of finding a child.

Gladys tells him it was this document that provided the date of the transaction, and the name and address of the buyers, which enabled her to find Hannah.

"You tell Mr. Parks what happened when I came to your house," she says, clutching her handbag on her lap.

Hannah smiles at Gladys shyly, and tells Mr. Parks that she was walking home one afternoon, after a long, tiring day at school—she teaches history, she informs him, at the high school for girls in Kimberley. She was carrying a heavy stack of exam papers that she was planning to mark that evening, when she saw someone sitting on the steps of her verandah.

It was a warm afternoon, the air dry. She was exhausted and discouraged by the difficulty of interesting the pupils she has in her class this year—a particularly rambunctious bunch, she explains—in the history which has always seemed so interesting to her. Also, she adds, she had recently had some unexpected expenses, having to repair the roof of the old house she had inherited.

Her adoptive parents, Lithuanian Jews, though they were much too careful to have left her any debts, had not been able to bequeath much money to keep up the old house and small back garden. With her pitiful teacher's salary, and despite her modest lifestyle, she is increasingly in debt. She is telling him this, she explains, lowering her gaze, not to complain or gain his sympathy, but so that he will understand her poor reception of Gladys, who was kind enough to come and seek her out and wait for her on her steps.

The thought of finding a beggar on her steps filled her with dismay. Raising a hand to her eyes, against the glare of the late afternoon light, to make out who was waiting for her, she was ready to send packing whoever it was. But, as she drew closer, she could see it was not a beggar at all. Hannah smiles at Gladys with a little sparkle in her brown eyes that Mr. Parks is beginning to find almost familiar.

He tells himself that if this is indeed the heiress they have been looking for, he would do well to treat her with some deference.

"Do go on," he says, giving her a small smile and stroking his mustache.

At first, she couldn't think what the elderly lady was doing at her house. She imagined she might be a religious zealot who wanted to sell her a tract and who might be even more difficult to shake off than any beggar.

She could see as she came closer that the woman was quite old—Hannah pulls a little apologetic face at Gladys—from the whiteness of the hair that emerged from the hat, and she felt even worse, thinking how difficult it would be to turn her away. She watched her rise with considerable difficulty, holding on to the railing of the steps with one gloved hand. She did, indeed, have a large black Bible in the other and had clearly been sitting there for some time.

Gladys stared at her, her gaze running over her like water. Mr. Parks, too, stares at the young woman now and imagines Gladys studying her short red curls, freckled forehead, and dark brown eyes, the small hands filled with books, the small feet in their dusty, flat shoes.

Then Gladys smiled at her with bright approval as though she had found what she had been looking for, and told her that she brought glad tidings: some very important news. Hannah still hesitated, taking all of this for a preamble to a religious imprecation. She had no wish to speak to anyone that day, and particularly not a Jehovah's Witness or someone of that sort who would talk to her about a miraculous message from God. But there was something about the look of recognition in her eyes, as though she somehow knew her, that made her feel obliged to ask her inside and to offer her a cup of tea.

Gladys sat down at her kitchen table. Hannah could feel her watch her curiously as she put on her old kettle and looked in her bare cupboards for a few biscuits.

Mr. Parks, at this point in the story, realizes he, too, should offer the ladies at least a cup of tea and sends his secretary off to prepare this. "Bring some biscuits, too," he adds.

"I'm afraid I didn't have much to offer you," Hannah says, smiling now at Gladys.

"Oh, I hadn't come for that kind of refreshment," she says.

While they were sitting opposite each other at the kitchen table over the weak cup of tea, with an old slice of lemon found at the bottom of the refrigerator drawer, and a few stale Marie biscuits, Gladys introduced herself and asked for Hannah's name.

"She asked me what the people who had brought me up had told me about my birth. I was taken aback by her question, but again I thought it was for religious reasons as she asked me in such a grave tone. There was no impertinence in her question. I said my guardians had told me nothing about my birth, only that I did not belong to them. Then she told me she thought she knew who my parents were and said we must come here to see you," Hannah says, and looks at him inquiringly with bright, intelligent eyes.

Gladys looks at her now, reaches across and lifts her trembling gloved hand to touch her cheek, as she asks Mr. Parks if he doesn't think she looks like her mother. "Yes, indeed," Mr. Parks admits. The frankness of her smile makes him think of Bill.

"Perhaps even more like her father," Gladys says as she cups Hannah's chin in her hand, strokes her hair. "Same red hair, dark eyes. Same sweet smile. Even the voice is similar," Gladys says, wonderment in her voice.

Mr. Parks, who cannot confirm this, never having met Isaac, now feels he must intervene. He says he will try to reach Mrs. McNulty again to see if she will confirm the story. He puts through the long distance call. This time, when he confronts the woman with the information he now possesses, what he is obliged to call a bill of sale, with her signature, she does not try to brush him off. When she hears that a considerable sum of money is involved in the inheritance, and finds out no one intends to prosecute her in any way, but rather to reward her for providing essential information, she recalls the details of the case, after all, and confesses to her rather lucrative part in the transaction. She explains that, left on her own by a husband who had gone off with everything she possessed, she was obliged to make a living for herself. "I believe I was of great help to some poor young women in trouble," she says.

He then turns to Hannah and says he is sorry to have to tell her that both her parents are dead. Her father had apparently died long ago, fighting in North Africa during the war, or so he was told by her mother's sisters when he questioned them, but her mother had been looking for her, before she died, and intended her to inherit most of her rather extensive estate.

Now that Hannah's identity has been confirmed to his satisfaction, he pours out the tea and hands Gladys a cup as well as Hannah. "Your madam would have been very grateful to you," he says, as he offers her one of her own biscuits. He tells the young woman he is very sorry he did not find her in time to take her to her mother.

He looks at Hannah now not without appreciation, as though in her small straw hat and her plain green dress, with its full skirt and narrow waist, her dusty shoes, and worn white gloves, she has acquired a glow.

In the end, Mr. Parks is moved to tell her that it must have been her baby girl, the child of her youth, her love child, who was the one she cared for more than anyone else in the world.

Acknowledgments

Again, I must thank my colleagues at Bennington and at Princeton, particularly Edmund White, for the story "In a Woman's Kingdom," and Joyce Carol Oates, for her support and encouragement; my editor at Penguin, Kathryn Court; my agent, Robin Straus; my three girls, Sasha, Cybele, and Brett, who have read and reread these pages; and always, my beloved husband, without whom none of this would have been possible.

A PENGUIN READERS GUIDE TO

LOVE CHILD

Sheila Kohler

An Introduction to
Love Child

"She thinks of the women in her life: her mother, her three maiden aunts, Gladys, her sisters, Helen. She has always been surrounded by women who kept secrets in shaded, silent places, but the secrets did not keep them" (p. 10).

At the age of forty-eight, Bill finds herself a wealthy widow. The splendor of her home and jewels, however, does not compensate for her loneliness. Shunned by polite Johannesburg society and effectively abandoned by her two teenage sons, she passes her days in an alcoholic fog. But when Bill's accountant, Mr. Parks, suggests she write a will, her reflections stir vivid memories of a youthful folly and the punishment that was exacted in its wake.

Bill's father was a South African diamond evaluator of British descent who "looked down on the Afrikaners" (p. 16) while working hard to support his wife and their four children. He doted on Bill, the family beauty, and relied upon her to help her hapless mother manage the household. Bill's mother, in turn, leveraged her husband's fondness for their middle daughter by sending her to fetch him back from the office whenever an "emergency" arose at home.

It was on one such excursion that Bill met Isaac. She'd already heard about her father's handsome co-worker from her sister Pie, who stifled her own attraction to Isaac because he was Jewish and she knew their father would never approve of him as a suitor. But at seventeen, Bill was bored. "She wanted excitement, even danger. She was restless and reckless. She wanted to fall in love" (p. 16).

After a brazen flirtation, Bill and Isaac began to meet in secret because of their differing faiths; "neither of them had dared to invite the other home" (p. 34). Certain that their families would relent once they were wed, the infatuated couple eloped to Kimberley, where Bill had three adoring maiden aunts who she was certain would help them. When none of the aunts agreed to stand witness to the marriage, Bill enlisted Gladys, her aunts' faithful mixed-blood servant, in their stead.

The newlyweds' romantic lark abruptly ended when Bill's parents arrived and insisted that the marriage be annulled. Flustered by her father's disapproval and her mother's tears, Bill allowed them to send Isaac away. After her parents' departure, Bill became a virtual prisoner in her aunts' genteel household. Gradually, Bill realized that she was suffering from morning sickness, and after the birth of her love child, the baby was taken away for adoption, to Bill's horror.

Both chilling and deeply moving, *Love Child* unravels the chain of events that led Bill from scandal to the gilded cage in which she resides thirty years later. In the exquisitely sparse yet evocative prose that has earned her international acclaim, Sheila Kohler crafts a haunting portrait of a woman whose life has been ruthlessly circumscribed by others and is now left to navigate the scant choices that remain.

About Sheila Kohler

Sheila Kohler was born in Johannesburg, South Africa. She received her undergraduate degree in literature from the Sorbonne, a graduate degree in psychology from the Institut Catholique, and an MFA in writing from Columbia University. Her work has won numerous awards and nominations, including two O. Henry Prizes, a Willa Cather Prize, and an Impac Award nomination. The film adaptation of her novel *Cracks*, starring Eva Green, will be released in March 2011. She teaches at Princeton University and Bennington College and lives in New York.

A CONVERSATION WITH
SHEILA KOHLER

Your last novel, Becoming Jane Eyre, *is about Charlotte Brontë and the writing of her timeless novel. Do you see Brontë and Bill as similar in any way? What drew you to each?*

There are some curious parallels between *Jane Eyre* and Bill's life, which is based to some extent on my mother's. Bill works in a family for a married man, as does Jane Eyre, and ends up marrying him. Of course, the mad wife in the attic is replaced in Bill's case by a very sane and intelligent wife, Helen. But Helen, too, suffers from a mysterious malady which Bill discovers after some time just as Jane discovers the existence of the real Mrs. Rochester.

Your prose is very lean, so one has the sense that every word is included for a reason. When Bill hides her jewels in a tin of Craven "A" cigarettes, are you deliberately evoking The Scarlet Letter? *Do various characters' references to* The Mill on the Floss, Jude the Obscure, *and* The Brothers Karamazov *hold any significance?*

I was definitely not thinking about any of these classical references, but I don't think we are always aware as writers what unconscious motives might make us choose a word, an image, or even a theme.

Except for the three sisters, all of the characters are rather conventionally named. Why did you choose to call them Pie, Bill, and Haze?

Pie and Haze are actually the names of my two aunts, and Bill is the nickname my mother was given. I was writing from life here entirely, though all the names seemed appropriate.

The names of the three maiden aunts, too, were from life: Maud, May, and Winnie, short for Winifred. Their story, of a father who leaves a will so that they cannot marry without relinquishing their income, is also drawn from life.

What initially inspired you to become a writer?

It is hard to say where the desire to write comes from, but certainly I was influenced by my aunt named Hazel in life and in the book, who read my sister, my cousin, and me the first chapter of *Jane Eyre* when I was seven years old. It made a tremendous impression on me and perhaps gave me the spark to try to do something similar of my own.

Your first story was published in 1987. How has your approach to the craft changed over time? Has writing become easier or more difficult?

I have learned, I believe, to have more confidence in myself as a writer and also, perhaps, to think of my reader more than I did initially. I'm not sure that the process has become any easier. Each time you go to the blank page the struggle begins again, though always for me with a kind of excitement and delight.

Is there a reason you set the novel in this time period? Was there anything of historical significance occurring at the time?

I used the period of my mother's life. So many things occurred during this time: two world wars, for example. But South Africa was removed and isolated to some extent from the great cataclysms of the time. However, I remember my mother saying that so much had changed during her lifetime, that so much had been invented: commercial airplane travel, for example.

Although you were born and raised in Johannesburg, South Africa, you have spent your adulthood living in Europe and the United States. Do you see yourself primarily as a South African writer? If so, what does that mean to you? If not, why are many of your books set there?

I suppose the place of childhood is particularly important in each writer's life. Though I was only there as a child, South Africa has continued to be a source of inspiration for me and I am currently embarked on a short story that takes place there. It is such a vivid place in so many ways: the bright sunlight, the luxuriant nature, and the juxtaposition of all this beauty with violence. Still, I don't think of myself as a South African writer but rather an immigrant writer, a *citoyenne du monde*, someone who doesn't really belong anywhere.

Bill has a mother who is ineffectual. How do you believe the lack of a strong maternal force influences a woman's future happiness?

This is the old question of nature and nurture, and the older I get the more I believe that we are born with a certain character and that life and our experiences—and our mothers, of course—alter this to some extent, but not irremediably for most of us. I have the feeling that Bill would have been who she was with or without the ineffectual mother.

As a teacher of writing, what are the most essential lessons that you try to communicate to your students?

I try to give my students the freedom to find their own voices and their own material and at the same time to teach them some basic elements of craft by suggesting they read the great masters and try to learn from them.

What do you see as the author's role in society?

An author's role is to make art, I believe, which concerns writing down the truths of life as he or she perceives them to the best of his or her ability and turning these truths into a story. If, out of this process, one is able to make people more aware of injustice in the society around us, that is certainly all to the better (one thinks of the great novels of Dickens, for example), but I don't think it can be our primary aim.

What are some of your favorite novels? Who are your literary influences?

Always such a difficult question to answer; I have so many favorite authors and so many influences. The great Russians: Chekhov, Dostoyevsky, and Tolstoy; the French, especially Flaubert's great novel, *Madame Bovary*, which is perhaps the perfect novel; and of course, my old English favorite, Dickens (I was very sad to hear from my students this semester that they had never read *David Copperfield* and had not made the acquaintance of Uriah Heep and Mr. Micawber); and of course the great women writers of the nineteenth century: George Eliot, Charlotte, Emily, and Anne Brontë. All these writers and many others have influenced me, and helped me, and I have been particularly inspired by my fellow countryman and Nobel prize winner, J. M. Coetzee, as well as my colleague Joyce Carol Oates.

What are you working on now?

I have just completed a draft of a novel called *The Bay of Foxes*. It is about a famous French writer (loosely modeled on Marguerite Duras) who disappears under mysterious circumstances. The novel is told from the point of view of a young Ethiopian aristocrat who works as the writer's secretary after she picks him up in a café in Paris. As in my novel *Cracks* there is a crime in the novel, and I found it very disturbing to write. It came to me unusually fast and took me to places where I have lived: Paris, Sardinia in the summer, and Rome.

QUESTIONS FOR DISCUSSION

1. Did your feelings about Bill change over the course of the novel? If so, how and why? If not, what was your initial opinion of her, and how was it confirmed?

2. Gladys "has lived her entire life vicariously through these white people" (p. 4), but outlives all three of Bill's maiden aunts and even Bill herself. What does her longevity represent?

3. Bill's father "loved his roses, which he tended and watered diligently, always muttering that no one should grow them in Africa, it was too difficult" (p. 15). What is the significance of his "roses"? What other metaphors does Kohler employ to describe her characters?

4. If Bill and Isaac had been allowed to marry, might they have found happiness together? Why or why not?

5. "She feels the terror and hurt in her life came when she allowed her family to penetrate her wall of protection, to be the authors of her story" (p. 51). Who is the "author" of Bill's story? What is the narrator's opinion of Bill?

6. Did Helen suspect that Bill would eventually relieve her of her unwanted sexual duties?

7. "She had seen men stare at her like this before, but that was not what he was looking for. He was looking for something particular" (p. 107). What is it that Mark is looking for in Bill?

8. Did Mark deliberately create a chasm between Bill and their sons? Would it have occurred to Mark that Bill would leave his wealth to someone besides their own children? Would he care?

9. When young Mark and Phillip return home for the Sunday visit immediately after Bill's disastrous appearance at their chapel, they gorge themselves on exactly the same meal that they rejected from their mother, "stuffing themselves with roast chicken and roast potatoes . . . to please the cook." What are some other instances in which Kohler uses food to tell a larger story?

10. Why is John, the Zulu cook, as devoted to Bill's boys as he is contemptuous of her? Why doesn't she dismiss him?

11. Do you read *Love Child* as ultimately tragic or hopeful?

12. Is this a story that could happen anywhere, or is the South African setting critical to the events of the novel?

For more information about or to order other Penguin Readers Guides, please e-mail the Penguin Marketing Department at reading@us.penguingroup.com or write to us at:

> Penguin Books Marketing Dept.
> Readers Guides
> 375 Hudson Street
> New York, NY 10014-3657

Please allow 4–6 weeks for delivery.
To access Penguin Readers Guides online, visit the Penguin Group (USA) Inc. Web site at www.penguin.com and www.vpbookclub.com.

AVAILABLE FROM PENGUIN

Becoming Jane Eyre
A Novel

ISBN 978-0-14-311597-7

PENGUIN
BOOKS

In a cold parsonage on the gloomy Yorkshire moors, a family seems cursed with disaster: a mother and two children dead, a father sick and without fortune, a son destroyed by alcohol and opiates, and three brilliant daughters reduced to poverty and spinsterhood with nothing to save them from their fate. Nothing, that is, except their remarkable literary talent. So unfolds the story of the Brontë sisters. Beautifully imagined, *Becoming Jane Eyre* delicately unravels the connections between one of fiction's most indelible heroines and the remarkable woman who created her.